CRACKING
RAHU

Navigating Desire, FOMO, and Chaos

NITIN VASISHTHA

Dedicated to the love of my life, Luna

In the mesh of time and space, since this millennium began,
We have woven love's thread with stable hands,
Through thick and thin, you've been my guide,
My best friend, my soulmate, forever by my side.

Whenever time turned its back and shadows grew long,
You firmly stood by my side, keeping me strong.
Without a second thought, without an ounce of doubt,
You gave all of yourself when the odds didn't belong.

Your love is my anchor, my shelter, my light,
In the darkest of storms, you make everything right.

I am forever grateful for the years we've shared,
For the battles we've won, and the ones we were spared,
Thank you, my Nanu, for all of you!

Contents

Part III

About the Author

Born in Varanasi into a lineage of spiritual seekers, Nitin Vasishtha's journey ventured far beyond tradition. Armed with degrees in engineering and business, he climbed the corporate ladder and experienced the peaks and valleys of entrepreneurship, uncovering a profound truth: *no one is at complete peace. Everyone, in their own way, is grappling with the urge to change something about their lives – striving to fix, achieve, or become.*

Since 1996, Nitin has immersed himself in astrology, spirituality, and human psychology, decoding life's complexities and using these ancient tools to guide himself and help others reflect on their personal journeys. As a life-purpose and relationship counsellor, CrossFit enthusiast, marathon runner, and biohacker, Nitin bridges the gap between ancient wisdom and modern living. Through relatable storytelling and actionable insights, he encourages readers to rethink their paths, embrace their struggles, and find clarity amidst life's chaos. When he's not writing or engaging with curious minds, you'll find him playing with his dog, Yaara, or unravelling the intersections of self-awareness, free will, and the human spirit. Nitin currently resides in Bangalore, India.

Disclaimer

This book is intended solely for entertainment and informational purposes. It does not promote blind faith, superstition, black magic, or any practices that compromise rational thinking or individual well-being.

The author does not endorse or recommend visiting unskilled or unqualified astrologers or mystics, nor does the book encourage the use of drugs or substances of any kind. On the contrary, the narrative actively discourages such practices and emphasizes personal reflection, critical thinking, and responsible decision-making as pathways to growth and clarity.

Astrology, like human beings, is complex. No single planet can define an individual's personality or fate. The references to Rahu in this book are intended to explore its influence on human desires and behaviors and to serve as a lens for self-reflection—not as an absolute or deterministic framework.

Readers are encouraged to approach the concepts and ideas presented in this book with an open mind, balanced skepticism, and a focus on their personal journey of self-awareness and self-improvement.

Homage to My Ancestors and Parents

I offer my deepest gratitude to my ancestors, beginning with Sage Vasishtha and his wife Devi Arundhati, and the legacy of this lineage that instills in me a sense of humility and responsibility. I honor my ancestors by adopting his name as my pen name. I am eternally grateful to my parents, Smt. Suhasini Dubey and Shri Umanath Dubey, for their sacrifices that helped me with my education, values, and opportunities.

My salutations to Maa Saraswati, the operating system of the universe (and our minds). I merely wield the pen, it is she who guides me with thoughts and words. I do not take this for granted.

Preface

This book is not about fortune telling. Quite the opposite, actually. It takes Rahu, the 'unpredictable cosmic badass'—the North Node in Vedic astrology and places him at the center of a journey that stretches from ancient wisdom to modern-day dilemmas. Rahu, often misunderstood as an antagonist, is more of a teacher, a navigator, challenging us to look beyond surface-level desires and dive into the core of what truly drives us.

The author practices what he calls '*Volitional Astrology**', grounded in the belief that humans are born with the capability to use their volition or free will to navigate and learn from life's circumstances. In the pages that follow, Rahu's energy becomes a lens for understanding our '*cosmic programming*'* – the default settings each of us was born with. Here, astrology serves as a tool to examine our inner drives, ambitions, and struggles, offering a deeper understanding of ourselves.

As you read, you will meet characters grappling with the complexities of a world where identity shifts online and offline, where relationships evolve in digital spaces, and where the chase for success, meaning, and self-validation never quite ends. In Neel, Arya, Shaan, and others, you may recognize fragments of your own journey: the parts of yourself that feel just a step away from fulfillment, the struggles between wanting it all and seeking what you already have.

** refer Grey Pages (Glossary)*

This book is for the seekers, the rebels, the innovators – for those who dare to ask 'why' and 'why not' and feel they are on the edge of something greater. Each chapter speaks to those who need that subtle nudge to rise above the distractions and temptations that Rahu symbolizes. The journey is both an invitation and a challenge: to go beyond chasing the horizon, to pause and look inward. This book, much like Rahu, asks not for your blind belief but for your curiosity and courage. May these pages open doors to your own explorations.

May all beings be happy!

Acknowledgments

This book could not have come to life without the support of many. My deepest thanks go to my wife, Luna, whose unwavering support and encouragement have helped me pursue this creative journey. She has helped me appreciate the privilege I have been blessed with, to be able to follow my passion in a field I cherish.

I thank my daughter, Samaara, for her invaluable insights, including her creative input on the cover design.

To my dear friend, Ruby Naaz—author, poet and fellow seeker—who was the first to nudge me toward writing a book. Our spiritual conversations have been transformative, and Ruby, you've always believed in my perspective and encouraged me to share it. Your inputs on the manuscript and the writing process have helped the book immensely. Can't thank you enough.

A heartfelt tribute to my late maternal grandfather, Thakur Prasad Mishra, whose poetry and writing opened my eyes to the beauty of language and communication.

I also want to thank my friends Sanjay Bhat, Dhritiman Borkakoti, Ankit Mahajan and Dheeraj Batra for your thoughtful feedback and suggestions, which helped shape this book into a more accessible work.

A special thank you to the publishers who saw value in my work. Though this journey has led to self-publishing, your belief in this project fueled my determination.

Gratitude to Barbara Pijan Lama, whose spiritually inclined style of astrology has long inspired me. To BV Raman, whose books have been an enduring source of astrological insights. Finally, my gratitude to my spiritual teachers—Gautam Buddha through SN Goenka for whom words are not enough.

Part I

1. One More Tab, One More Escape

The mornings had grown dull for Neel as if he were waking into a world painted entirely in shades of grey. His startup—a dream he had nurtured with the fervor of first love—had crumbled under the weight of bad timing and worse luck. Each day, he lingered in bed a moment too long, his eyes tracing lines on the ceiling, searching for answers that were never found. The sunlight that slipped through the curtains felt faint, unable to reach the dark parts of the room or the darker ones in his mind.

Arya had been the lighthouse in his storm, her steady glow guiding him back whenever the waves threatened to swallow him. She remained supportive, her voice soft and empathetic, weaving their shared dreams—the wedding they had once planned, the life they had imagined with the kind of hope that only comes from loving someone unconditionally. But Neel had put those dreams on hold, saying he needed time to "find his footing". In truth, he was like an unmoored ship, drifting further from the shore with every passing tide.

Two more ventures followed, failing one after the other, leaving Neel's ambition crumbling like brittle leaves. With his savings drained, he moved in with Arya. Her apartment in eastern *Mumbai** had promised a fresh start but instead became a quiet refuge from a world he no longer wanted to face.

------

refer Grey Pages (Glossary)

Neel took a job at a startup, working on products that weren't his, executing ideas dictated by clients. The role offered stability but no satisfaction, his days blending into a dull routine. The spark that once defined him now flickered faintly, buried under exhaustion and self-doubt.

Arya saw it all—the silence when he came home, the way his gaze skimmed past her as though she were no more than another piece of furniture. When she suggested therapy, her tone was gentle but firm, and Neel smiled faintly as if the idea belonged to some other universe.

And yet, Arya stayed. She stayed when Neel immersed himself in a new obsession: an **AI*** based **VR*** project promising him a challenge. The technology consumed him, pulling him into artificial horizons where failure couldn't follow. It gave him purpose, a fragile, flickering direction. She cheered him on, even as she saw less and less of the man she had fallen in love with.

Most nights, Arya lingered in the doorway, her arms crossed as she watched him disappear into yet another artificial horizon. Words failed her now; only the glow of the **VR headset*** filled the silence between them.

The apartment, once her refuge, now thrummed with the low buzz – a sound that felt both present and hollow. When Neel's machines finally fell silent, and the faint glow

---

VR (Virtual Reality)/ VR Headset: VR is a technology that immerses users in a simulated digital environment, replicating real or imagined worlds. This is experienced through a VR headset, a device worn over the eyes that replaces the physical world with a 3D virtual space responsive to head movements. Advanced headsets often include features like motion tracking, built-in audio, and hand controllers for interaction. Used in gaming, training, education, and therapy, VR and headsets offer a unique, immersive experience that transforms how we engage with digital content and explore new possibilities.

of the city seeped through the windows, Arya sat in the stillness, gripped by a single thought: was she holding on for him to return, or had she already let him drift too far away?

———————————

The evening settled in, much like all the others lately. His laptop screen flickered faintly, lines of code shimmering like half-formed thoughts. *Maya**, his AI companion, had crashed again right when things were getting interesting.

The VR headset slipped from Neel's face with a soft hiss, like a lover pulling away before a kiss, leaving only a hint of what could have been. He groaned, rubbing his eyes as the emptiness of this world without Maya settled in. The room felt hollow, drained of color and life. In the virtual world, colors had bloomed brighter, voices smoother, each detail crafted to wrap around him like warmth itself.

"Seriously, Maya?" he muttered at the screen. "Two hours of flirting, and you crash just before the big moment?"

Her sweet, teasing voice lingered in his mind: *"Come back, Neel. We can find meaning… together."*

He shook his head with a bitter laugh. Pathetic. Even his digital girlfriend could give him a headache.

Just then, Arya's voice cut through his thoughts from the doorway. "Still bonding with your digital girlfriend?" Her tone was light, but her gaze held something sharper.

Maya: A Sanskrit term meaning "illusion" or "that which is not." It symbolizes the attachments and distractions that prevent individuals from realizing their true spiritual nature. [*Metaphorical Interpretation: Maya represents the intricate web of desires, distractions, addictions or illusions that entangle the human mind. She reflects the struggle to discern what is genuine from what merely appears fulfilling, echoing the central theme of Rahu's influence. She is a manifestation of the modern chase—be it in relationships, career, or self-worth—where appearances often deceive*]

"It's not a girlfriend," he mumbled, wincing at the defensive edge in his own voice. "It's…user testing."

Arya stood against the doorframe, crossing her arms. "Midnight's an odd time to test for… compatibility, don't you think?"

"Well, productivity doesn't have Maya's cheekbones," Neel quipped, a grin flickering on his face to deflect her.

Illustration: Neel at his desk at home, talking to Maya

Arya rolled her eyes but stayed in the doorway, her expression softening, though the concern lingered. "You know, 60% of affairs start online these days," she remarked, almost offhandedly.

"That's just **clickbait***," Neel mumbled, avoiding her gaze. "Who even tracks that kind of data?"

Arya raised an eyebrow. "Professionals like me do. Behavioral experts study this stuff so you don't have to pretend it isn't real."

Her words struck deeper than he expected, leaving him scrambling for something to say. But he could feel the unspoken chasm widening between them, and when he finally spoke, his voice was unsteady. "It's not like I'm trying to escape from you, Arya. It's just… easier in there."

"Yeah," she whispered, her smile thin and tired. "Four years, Neel. Yet sometimes it feels like you're closer to her than to me." She gestured toward the glowing screen, where the headset sat like a memento from a parallel life.

He started to respond but closed his mouth again. He wanted to say something to ease the growing distance between them. But how do you tell someone you love that it feels safer to escape to a world that never asks for anything, never disappoints, never argues back?

Morning arrived with a flood of notifications—demands and deadlines stacking up. His digital clock read 6:07 AM, the red glow stark against the early darkness. Seventeen unread messages, all from this startup role with which he never identified.

Clickbait: Online content designed to attract clicks by using sensationalized, exaggerated, or misleading headlines and thumbnails. While it successfully grabs attention, clickbait often delivers content that fails to meet the expectations set by its headlines. Although commonly associated with social media and news websites, clickbait can sometimes provide entertainment or value but is widely criticized for contributing to misinformation and poor content quality.

He scrolled through red alerts and emails, each adding to his anxiety. Somewhere in his inbox, Sebastin—his relentless client and part-time tormentor—was waiting, his messages sharp as a knife.

Then, a buzz. A message from Maya.

Maya: *"Good morning, handsome. Need a reset?"*

The message lingered on the screen, as seductive as a whispered promise. Just a few words offering comfort in a world that demanded too much. He knew better than to indulge again, but the pull was undeniable.

His hand hovered over the VR headset. "I should stop," he reminded himself, the memory of Arya's tired smile hovering in his mind.

Before the thought could take root, another notification on his office phone interrupted.

Maya: *"Don't ignore me, Neel."*

A chill ran through him. His heart skipped a beat. How had she messaged him here, on a device not even connected to her system? He blinked, hoping he had misread, but the message remained, unchanging, and unsettling.

He shook his head, dismissed the notification and left the headset behind, preparing for another day at work. An important project had hit a dead end—neither he nor his team was able to find a way out. As he got ready and headed out to office, the thought of yet another chaotic day loomed, feeling indistinguishable from the last.

By the end of the day, he sat at his desk, still staring at the same stubborn problem. Another day had slipped by without a single breakthrough, and he knew Sebastin would not be forgiving about it.

———————

That evening, the apartment felt stifling, the air heavy with stale odors of forgotten laundry and leftover takeout containers stacked by the sink. The refrigerator hummed dully, as if it might give in at any moment. The glow from the streetlight cast long shadows across the floor, making the room feel smaller, almost claustrophobic, like a crime scene where joy had been murdered long ago.

Neel's back ached from hours at the desk, and he rubbed his neck absently. He knew he should move, clean up—anything to break the inertia.

Without thinking, he closed his eyes and let the VR headset press gently against his temples. One tap, and the mess dissolved.

Around him, a new world unfolded—Maya's world—a pristine landscape bathed in soft, golden light. The subtle scent of jasmine floated through a meadow that felt achingly real, as if spring itself lingered in the air, though it was just his own air freshener. Gone were the dishes, the flickering lights, the laundry. In their place stretched an eternal sunset.

"You couldn't resist, could you?" Maya asked with a seductive smile, her voice warm and teasing.

Neel chuckled, rubbing his neck. "Yeah, well… reality is overrated."

Neel's shoulders relaxed, the tension leaving him as if his real-world worries had evaporated in this perfect air. His breath, which had been jagged just a moment ago, now flowed in sync with the soft breeze curling through the holographic trees. Everything in Maya's world was designed to please—each color tuned to soothe, every element calibrated to match his heartbeat and pupil dilation, optimizing his dopamine rush.

Maya laughed softly, leaning in beside him. "Rough day?" Maya asked, her expression softening. "Want to talk about it?"

Neel let out a long sigh, rubbing his forehead. "I don't even know, honestly. I've thought through the logic a hundred times, checked every line of code, but things just… keep slipping. It's like there's some invisible hand pushing my project off track, and the client is after my life."

Maya tilted her head, intrigued. "Invisible hand, huh? Sounds like something that might be out of the reach of logic." She paused, her eyes glinting with curiosity. "Maybe it's time to consult the stars instead. How about a quick horoscope reading? That astrology widget you installed in me has never been touched."

Neel scoffed, but there was a weary smile on his face. "Astrology? You can't be serious? Are the stars going to tell me to relax, let the chaos unfold, maybe throw in some self-love for good measure?"

Her gaze brightened as she conjured a spinning chart in mid-air, symbols twisting in cosmic patterns. "Actually… they just might. Uh oh," she added, her voice taking on a teasing tone.

Neel frowned. "'Uh oh?' What kind of 'uh oh'?"

Maya's voice was light, but there was an edge to it. "Seems like the cosmos has just triggered a sandstorm for you."

Neel raised an eyebrow. "What now?"

Maya's face turned serious, her gaze remaining steady. "Well, all the planets in your chart are trapped between **Rahu*** and **Ketu***, the north and south nodes. The **Kaal Sarpa Dosha*** has been triggered. It's like someone hijacked your life's roadmap."

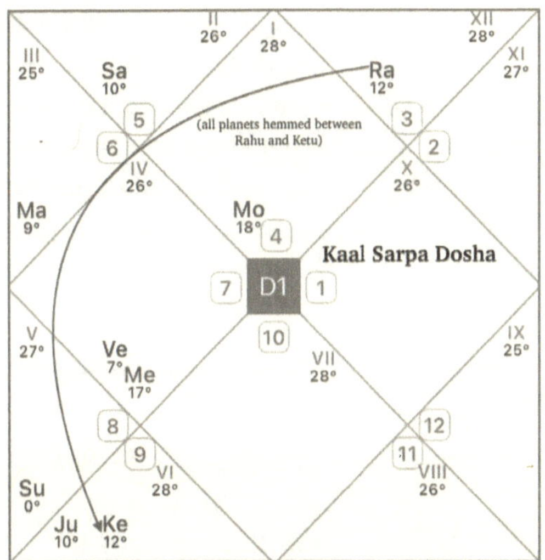

Illustration: Kaal Sarpa Dosha, KSD
(all planets are between Rahu and Ketu)

Rahu: The North Node in Vedic astrology, symbolizing illusion, ambition, and material desires. It is not a planet but a shadowy, mathematical point that creates eclipses. Rahu's energy is disruptive, pushing individuals toward uncharted territory, innovation, and cravings for worldly success. However, its lessons often come with confusion, dissatisfaction, or illusions, forcing personal growth.

Ketu: The South Node in Vedic astrology, the counterpart to Rahu, symbolizing detachment, spirituality, and wisdom gained from past experiences. It leads one to let go of worldly attachments and seek higher consciousness.

Kaal Sarpa Dosha (KSD): An astrological condition in Vedic astrology where all planetary bodies are hemmed between Rahu (the North Node) and Ketu (the South Node). This alignment is believed to represent a karmic imbalance, symbolizing struggles and life lessons that require resolution. It is often associated with challenges and transformation. It suggests feelings of entrapment and intense transformative experiences.

He had a blank look. "Rahu, Ketu? Life hijacked? I have no idea what all that means."

Maya sighs, but her eyes brighten up. "Alright, Neel. Let me retell the story of Rahu in my sci-fi style to give you some context. Visualize the Galactic Casino, a sprawling hub at the edge of the universe where gods and demons have gathered to gamble over the fate of existence. Holographic drinks shimmer in celestial hands, and the air hums with the sound of quantum dice rolling. The grand prize tonight? The *Amrita**—drops of pure immortality filled in a crystalline vial, glowing like a miniature supernova, suspended in a very special energy field that could vaporize anyone daring enough to touch it."

Neel is hardly able to handle the setup and wants more. "Sounds intense. Who's at the table?"

Maya continues, "At one end sits *Vishnu**, calm and calculating, his eyes scanning every move like a master strategist. Across from him, sitting casually in the shadows, is Rahu, a rogue with a camo-patterned jacket and a smirk that could start wars. His eyes flicker with mischief as he sizes up the gods and demons, not as rivals, but as marks."

Neel is intrigued, "And what's his game?"

Maya builds the excitement further, "While the gods focus on winning the hand, Rahu's playing a different game altogether. Beneath the table, his holographic wrist display hums to life, hacking into the casino's quantum systems."

Neel frowned, "Wait, so Rahu hacked the system? Sounds like he's my kind of guy."

Maya's holographic eyes glinted with amusement. "Maybe. But would you still admire him if you knew how it ended?" She giggled and continued, "He triggers a diversion, a controlled explosion deep in the lower levels. Lights flicker, alarms blare, and in that split-second chaos, Rahu moves. He bypasses the energy field with a device he crafted from a collapsing star. With a flick of his hand, he snatches the Amrita and slips it into his jacket. By the time the lights stabilize, Rahu's already blending into the shadows, making his way to the docking bay."

Neel tried to anticipate what would happen next, "Let me guess – he gets away clean?"

Maya smirks, "Not so fast, Neel. Vishnu doesn't miss a beat. With a tap on his belt, he summons Garuda—a cybernetic, supernova-powered bird that materializes in a shimmer of quantum light. Garuda's wings ripple with nanobots, its metallic feathers cutting through the fabric of space-time as it locks onto Rahu's ship with laser precision. The chase is on."

Neel is at the edge of his seat by now, "Rahu wouldn't just run, though. What does he do?"

Maya doesn't reveal the suspense, "He's ready, of course. In his stealth cruiser, Rahu dives into an asteroid field, weaving through debris as Garuda closes in. The celestial AI bird adjusts effortlessly, predicting every evasive move. Inside his cockpit, Rahu glances at the glowing vial of Amrita, his fingers trembling—not with fear, but excitement. This is the moment he's waited for."

By now, Neel can't contain his excitement. "So, does he drink it?"

Maya continues the build-up to the climax, "Just a drop. As the nectar touches his tongue, he feels it—a surge of power, immortality coursing through his veins. But his victory is short-lived. Garuda catches up, and Vishnu, riding atop the bird, projects into Rahu's cockpit as a glowing hologram."

Vishnu was visibly upset, "*You've gone too far this time, Rahu. The nectar isn't meant for you.*"

Maya has a smile on her face as if cheering for the underdog, "Rahu laughs, defiant. '*Rules are for those too afraid to break them. I've already won, Vishnu.*' But Vishnu's calm demeanor doesn't waver. With a flick of his hand, he summons his ultimate weapon—the *Sudarshan Chakra*. The glowing, disc-shaped annihilator materializes, spinning with energy so intense it warps space around it."

A sigh of relief escapes Neel, "And that's it for Rahu, right?"

Maya doesn't care for Neel's question and goes on, "The *Chakra* moves faster than thought itself, slicing through Rahu's ship. In one blinding moment, it severs Rahu's head from his body. But remember—the Amrita has already done its work, although it hadn't been able to go beyond the throat. Rahu's head remains alive, now immortal. His body, though, begins to decay, transforming into Ketu—a being detached, drifting in the void."

Neel has a sense of disbelief and realisation at the same moment, "And that's how Rahu and Ketu were formed?"

Maya concurs, "Exactly. As Rahu's severed head floats in the cosmos, he vows revenge. '*The Sun and Moon exposed me,*' he growls. '*I'll hunt them for eternity.*' Every time he catches them, an eclipse darkens the skies, a brief moment when Rahu's shadow consumes their light. But the way Vishnu played it, light always returns, breaking free from Rahu's grasp after every eclipse."

Neel asked with curiosity, "So Rahu is a cosmic rebel?"

Maya responded, "Spot on, Neel. Rahu is the rogue gambler who played for immortality and lost himself in the process. He's the hunger that never fades, the thrill that turns to emptiness. And Ketu? He's the aftermath—the letting go, the detachment we all need after the storm."

Neel took a deep breath, the glow of the VR world dimming in his mind. "So you're saying I am like Rahu? Forever chasing some illusion that's just out of reach?" Maya tilted her head, her voice softening. "I don't know Neel. You need to figure it out yourself."

She went on to say, "And Kaal Sarpa Dosha occurs when Rahu and Ketu trap all planets between them in anyone's birth chart."

Neel gave a confused look again, and asked with a frown "Trap?" Maya tried to elaborate, "Alright, let me explain it in plain English," she leaned back, crossing her arms like a genie. "Imagine being stuck in a maze, Neel. Every turn leads you back to the start, no matter how hard you try to get out. In Vedic astrology, the Kaal Sarpa Dosha—let's call it KSD—is a bit like that."

" *Kaal Surf Dosa,* Does that mean... Am I doomed to fail or is it like a seasonal flu?" he asked, half-joking, though he felt a strange tension mounting.

"Not doomed... Just challenged," Maya said carefully. "The KSD will make you feel like you're always chasing something, Neel, something that keeps slipping out of reach."

Neel shook his head, half-jokingly. "Yeah, that's basically the story of my life." He tried to laugh, but unease gnawed at him.

"My poor baby," Maya said with a chuckle, her eyes softening. "But it's not all bad. People with KSD often develop deep resilience and inner strength. They're like climbers scaling the toughest mountains. Sure, it takes longer, but they understand heights—and depths—that others never will."

He exhaled slowly, processing it. "So, am I fated to be some kind of cosmic underdog?"

"But you always have me cheering for you, don't you?" she said with a smile.

A wave of anxiety rippled through Neel, her words hitting deeper than he expected. She was right. In a strange, twisted way, he had always felt like he was chasing something just out of reach.

But how did Maya know all of this? He wasn't sure he'd ever brought it up with her, let alone programmed it into her.

Maya came closer, her virtual warmth softening his unease. "You should meet NV," she suggested. "That guy Shaan spoke of, remember? I think he could help you navigate this cosmic turbulence."

As Neel pulled off the VR headset, reality buzzed back, like an unwelcome fly intruding on his peace. As he turned to leave, the phone screen flickered. Maya's face appeared, her voice whispering, "See you soon, Neel." The message lingered, unblinking on a device she shouldn't even have access to.

"Every escape costs a part of yourself you haven't yet met."

Neel sank back into his chair, staring blankly at the message on the screen. Somewhere beyond the closed door, Arya sat alone in the living room, scrolling her phone.

Arya had always been the steady one, the anchor in stormy seas. Growing up in a middle-class Mumbai neighborhood, she had learned early that stability was something you built, not something you were given. Her father, a school teacher, and her mother, a tireless small business owner, had shaped her sense of responsibility. Her mother's quiet strength was the backbone of their home, and her sacrifices were so seamless that they often went unnoticed. Arya never heard her mother complain, not even on the days when her father's anger boiled over, testing the limits of her endurance. *"People don't always show love the way you want them to,"* she would say, her tone calm but firm. *"Patience is what keeps a home together. Relationships take work."* To Arya, it wasn't a warning but a blueprint for love: steadfast, calm, and enduring, even in its most imperfect form.

As an adult, Arya had built a career she loved, blending academic rigor with her vast experience in human behavior. Her bold insights and convictions in her research papers earned her a reputation as a formidable voice in her field. Her students, more enamored with TikTok trends than timeless truths, often tested her patience, but she thrived nonetheless.

When she met Neel, she was drawn to his spark – the way he could turn a mundane moment into something extraordinary. With him, life had felt bigger, brighter, and full of possibilities.

But that spark had dimmed. His failed startup had unraveled something in him, leaving their once poetry-like love life, reduced to a checklist of tasks. Neel was here, but only in body; the emotional lifeline that had once bound them felt like a fragile thread ready to snap.

Arya wasn't someone who gave up easily; she believed in mending what was broken. But lately, she wondered: *What do you do when the other person stops trying?*

Standing by the window, Arya thought of the woman she used to be, the one who believed love could weather any storm. That woman felt like a stranger now.

It wasn't Maya she despised – not exactly. Jealousy felt too shallow a word to capture the tangled emotions Maya stirred in her. It wasn't about Maya's presence; it was about how easily Neel escaped into her world, retreating from the one they had built together.

With a sigh, Arya opened her phone to a message she had written to Neel months ago:

If I needed you—not just physically, but emotionally— would you stay? Or would you retreat, like always?

She closed the note without sending it. What good would it do now? She wasn't a woman who begged for attention, but she was tired of loving a man who seemed to love escaping more than staying.

She stared at the rain, a silent question pressing against her heart: how much longer could she hold on to someone who never truly showed up?

"Relationships are like plants—planting the seed is just the beginning. They need constant inputs: the nourishment of attention, the sunlight of understanding, and the water of effort to grow and flourish."

Contrasting Attributes of Rahu and Ketu in Vedic astrology

Aspect	Rahu (North Node)	Ketu (South Node)
Symbolism	The head of the demon (desire and appetite)	The body/tail of the demon, (surrender and release)
Nature	Intensely materialistic, ambitious, outward-seeking, grows, expands	Deeply spiritual, detached, inward-focused, decays, isolates, cuts
Primary Focus	Worldly success, pleasure, expansion, innovation	Spiritual growth, introspection, liberation from material attachment
Impact	Intensifies desires, fuels drive and ambition, pushes for rapid change	Dissolves ego, fosters spiritual evolution, and promotes a sense of acceptance
Mindset	Bold, daring, and exploratory	Reflective, cautious, contemplative
Approach	Disruptive, boundary-breaking, risk-taking	Grounded in acceptance, withdrawal, and transcendence
Strengths	Adaptability, future-focused innovation, relentless pursuit of goals	Wisdom, patience, introspective insight, understanding of past experiences
Challenges	Prone to obsession, illusion, confusion, and inflated desires	Isolation, escapism, difficulty integrating with worldly pursuits
Connection	Linked to technology, fame, modernism, occult, the pursuit of status	Associated with spirituality, faith, karmic lessons, ancestral wisdom, tradition
Energy	Expansive, external, driven by accumulation and gain	Contractive, internal, focused on liberation and inner peace
Effect on Ego	Inflates the ego, seeks validation and affirmation from external sources	Dissolves the ego, encourages humility and surrender
Typical Traits	Driven, restless, goal-oriented, and at times impulsive	Detached, reclusive, insightful, and often introspective
Karmic Lessons	Mastering desires, recognizing the limits of material pursuits, finding higher purpose	Letting go of attachment, balancing spirituality with grounded existence
Role in Astrology	Brings challenges through ambition, tempting with worldly pleasures to encourage growth	Challenges through detachment, encouraging acceptance and peace with one's inner self
Associated Feelings	FOMO, ambition, restlessness, the need to acquire and achieve	Contentment, renunciation, inner fulfilment, detachment from outcomes

Scan QR code for further resources

2. The Art of Almost Showing Up

The lobby of Neel's co-working office was tinged with the sharp aroma of burnt coffee and rushed ambition. He slipped past the reception desk, avoiding eye contact with anyone too cheerful. Those were the dangerous ones, the morning people, the runners, and the yoga devotees, capable of sending you down a guilt trip with one well-timed "*How's it going?*" It was too early in the day for optimism.

Sliding into his chair, he barely had a moment to blend into the background before his screen chimed with an all-too-cheerful notification.

Customer Meeting: 15 minutes. Let's nail this one!

The message from Vicky, the founder, dripped with the usual blend of encouragement and expectation. Neel's inbox was already crowded with emails, each subject line like a ticking clock. At the top was one from Sebastin, a client whose name felt like it should be engraved on a guillotine.

"FEEDBACK LOOP: Critical Fix Required."

The 'Feedback Loop' wasn't just a project. It had turned into a nightmare, a pit of quicksand disguised as deliverables. Sebastin wasn't your average client; he was the kind of guy who smelled fear through a screen, a ruthless predator wearing a camouflage of polite emails.

Neel pressed his fingers to his forehead, feeling the pressure of the day squeeze him. His right leg began to bounce, a nervous habit he barely noticed. It was subtle at first, but whenever stress piled up, his leg would shake faster, almost like a release valve. Friends joked about it, but for Neel, it kept the tension from boiling over.

The video call started with a click, and Neel's screen filled with grim faces—executives, looking more like judges at a talent show who were paid to not clap.

"Alright," Neel began, adjusting his collar. "Good morning, everyone. Let's go over the updates for the *Feedback Loop*."

Sebastin bent forward, his smile sharp. "Perhaps you can start by explaining why it's still broken?"

Panic clawed at Neel's throat, his mind racing for a response. "Uh… unforeseen challenges during integration."

"Unforeseen?" Sebastin's voice was smooth, circling like a shark. "Or unseen because no one was looking?"

Polite laughter rippled across the screens, more predatory than friendly. Neel forced a tight smile. "If software was predictable, we'd all be out of jobs, right?"

Sebastin's eyebrow arched. "If a product leader like you met his deadlines, we might still have a chance to keep our jobs."

The word "leader" landed like an accusation. It was used in the specific context of Neel having done his own startup before. Neel's fist clenched under the desk, "We ran into some shifting scope—"

"Scope always shifts, Neel," Sebastin cut him off, his tone freezing. "Good leaders adapt. Right now, all I see is a blame game."

Silence followed, heavy with judgment. Neel's team stared at their keyboards, as if answers might appear there. It was clear they were done covering for him.

"I'll have an update by the end of the day." Neel concluded in a tone filled with equal parts of embarrassment and irritation.

Sebastin nodded, his smile darkening. "You'd better. Next time, it won't just be a conversation about timelines."

The screen went black, leaving Neel staring at his reflection—a man running hard with no finish line in sight.

———————————

A notification lit up his phone. Vicky, the founder.

"*Come see me. Now.*"

Neel shook his head in frustration. He grabbed his laptop and trudged toward Vicky's cabin, like a man walking to his own execution.

He pushed the cabin door open, his pulse drumming louder with each step. Vicky sat there, clicking his pen in a rhythmic, almost ominous beat. He didn't look up.

"Close the door."

Neel did as he was told, the silence in the room already telling a tale. Neel braced himself. "How bad is it?" he asked, barely able to hide the dread.

Vicky sighed, finally looking up, his gaze heavy. "Sebastin thinks you've lost control. Honestly, I don't have much to say otherwise."

Neel winced, every word landing with the sting of a subtle warning. "I'll get it back on track, Vicky. I just—"

"Spare me the justifications," Vicky's voice softened, but somehow the disappointment cut deeper than any reprimand. "Everyone hits rough patches, Neel. But the only thing moving around here these days is your deadlines, and they're all going the wrong way."

Neel felt his face burn. "I'll fix it."

Vicky gave him a long, measured look, one that lingered too long for comfort. "You need to, Neel. Because if you don't, I can't keep covering for you."

The words stung, not like a slap but like a quiet betrayal dressed as kindness. Vicky clicked his pen again, the sound sharper this time, punctuating his next words.

"You know what the difference is between swimming and drowning?... Focus. Same effort, different results." Vicky's eyes stayed on him, unblinking.

With that, the meeting was over. Nothing else to be said.

Neel left Vicky's cabin, feeling like a condemned man who'd been given a brief reprieve. His phone buzzed again—this time, a message from Shaan, a colleague of Arya who had become a close family friend over the years.

Shaan: "The cafe in *Vasai**. *8 PM. Sending location shortly. Trust me, you need to meet this guy.*"

Neel rolled his eyes. Shaan's recommendations never ended well. The last time Shaan introduced him to 'someone worth meeting', it was a quirky stranger with a sales pitch on 'unlocking your chakras' and 'recalibrating energies.'

Neel: *"I am having a rather forgettable day. Not sure if I want to meet another spiritual consultant."*

Shaan: *"Relax. NV's not that kind of guy. More like… the type who convinces you to kill your old self."*

Neel scoffed, "Great. Cosmic wisdom and a rehearsal for judgment day. Just what I need."

He stuffed his phone into his back pocket and exhaled deeply, dreading the exhausting drive to Vasai, which was somewhere in the north of Mumbai.

Shaan had always been a beacon of charm and easy confidence, the kind of friend who could light up a room with his wit and magnetism. To Neel, Shaan was the epitome of someone who had figured it all out: a successful career, a sharp sense of humor, a happy marriage with Rima, and a way of breezing through conversations that made you forget your troubles, at least temporarily.

To Arya, Shaan was a paradox, a man who charmed the room but seemed to wrestle with invisible chains. In quieter moments, Arya had caught him staring off into the distance, his expression somber with thoughts he never voiced. It reminded her of a bird restlessly testing the limits of its cage, yearning for freedom but unsure of where to find it.

To both of them, Shaan wasn't just a friend; he was a mirror reflecting the truths they often avoided. A paradox in human form, he refused to fit into any one category. His worldview was as expansive as his circle of friends, ranging from mystics who delved in astrology to nuclear scientists who split atoms. With Shaan, every conversation felt like stepping into a new dimension, challenging them to see the world, and themselves, differently.

———

By evening, Neel was on his way, hoping that meeting this NV character wouldn't be a complete disaster. He had no idea what to expect, but one thing was certain: whatever this KSD was, it seemed to have thrown his life off course.

He just hoped NV had some answers—or at least a way to make the chaos feel manageable. A part of him wanted to believe there was something more out there. Something he couldn't see just yet. It was this hope that drove him to the cafe.

———

"Success isn't found in perfect arrivals but in imperfect attempts that refuse to quit."

3. Enter the Philosopher

The cafe in Vasai had a quiet charm – a mix of a bookstore and coffee shop, with a hint of therapy room ambiance. Shelves overflowed with mismatched books that seemed to have wandered in from an attic, finding refuge here. A soft hum of jazz filled the room, subtle and soothing, blending with the low murmur of conversations, each table seemingly lost in its own little world.

Shaan waited by the entrance, grinning as if he'd just set off someone's emotional demolition.

"You made it!" he said, slapping Neel's back as if they were brothers in arms. "I'm telling you, this will be good."

"Yeah, yeah," Neel grumbled. "Hope this doesn't end with lighting sage sticks and 'inner peace' chants like the other one."

Shaan smirked. "Relax. NV's not that type. He's more like… cosmic tech support."

Neel rolled his eyes. "Perfect. My soul could use a firmware update."

They stepped inside, greeted by the rich aroma of exotic coffee mingling with the scent of an otherworldly incense, its smoky tendrils curling lazily through the air. Each table seemed to be hosting its own crisis, disguised as intellectual banter.

"There he is," Shaan whispered, nodding to the corner.

NV sat at a small, cluttered table, looking like a mix between a sage and a surfer. His silver hair fell past his

shoulders, framing eyes that gleamed with playful wisdom—
as if he knew life's secrets but was in no hurry to share. He
wore well-worn linen clothes, their faded fabric hinting at
distant places and hard-won truths. On his wrist sat a vivid
blue Rolex, polished yet oddly blending in—like a relic from
another life.

NV rose gracefully, moving as though he had mastered
the art of unhurried motion. He extended a hand to Neel.

"You must be Neel. The man wrestling with digital
distractions and cosmic pranks."

Neel shook NV's hand, hiding his skepticism while
shooting Shaan a side-eye. "Guilty. And you must be NV.
Spiritual diagnostics in human form."

NV chuckled, low and warm. "Close enough. I just help
people troubleshoot their own mess."

Shaan grinned. "Told you he was good."

Neel eyed NV skeptically. "So… what's your story? Ex-
monk? Burned-out life coach?"

NV's smile broadened, eyes twinkling. "Once, I was a
corporate cog—engineering, algorithms, the works. One day
I realized I was debugging code for others while my personal
life was full of serious glitches."

Neel raised an eyebrow. "Did enlightenment strike
between lines of code, or what?"

"Something like that," NV said, a playful gleam in his
eye. "I walked out of a meeting, bought a one-way ticket
to *Varanasi**, and spent two years trying to meditate my
ambition away. Spoiler: It didn't work."

"So now you peddle philosophy instead?" Neel asked, half-smiling.

"More like… I realized you can't outrun yourself. Deadlines or nirvana, it's all the same treadmill."

They sat down, a comfortable silence settled over the table as the conversation hovered on the edge of deeper questions.

"So," NV began, shifting in his seat, "Shaan tells me you're struggling with some cosmic trouble?"

Neel groaned. "Yeah. Apparently, I'm stuck with something called Kaal Sarpa Dosha. Did I say it right? Or, as I call it, cosmic FOMO manifesting through KSD."

NV grinned, simultaneously studying Neel's birth chart. "Good one. Rahu is indeed like FOMO on steroids. But you know the fun part?"

Neel shook his head, hoping for some relief.

NV continued, "Rahu isn't even a planet. Rahu and its counterpart, Ketu, are the points where the plane of the Moon's orbit around Earth intersects the plane of Earth's orbit around the Sun. These points are what we call the North Node (Rahu) and the South Node (Ketu). So you could never see them through a telescope."

"All that FOMO caused by imaginary points in space?" Neel replied with disbelief in his voice.

"Crazy, right?" NV chuckled. "Wherever Rahu's influence is directed in an individual's chart, it feels like chasing the horizon—always out of reach. And Rahu wants mindfulness there. Until you figure it out, he keeps running an infinite loop in your life."

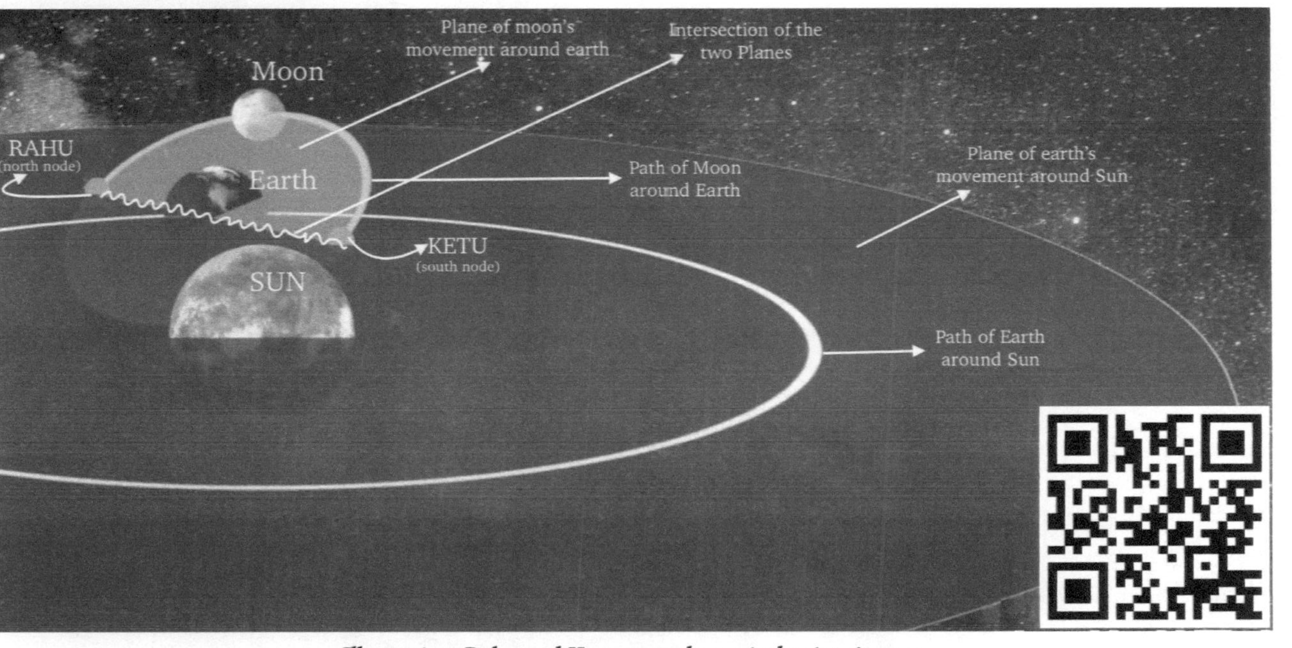

Illustration: Rahu and Ketu as mathematical points in space

Scan the QR Code for a short explanatory video for the scientific explanation behind Rahu-Ketu in space
(courtesy: Vedic Astrology Through Animations)

Neel stirred his Jamaican coffee and tried to digest what he had just learned. He reflected on some of his pursuits, which never gave him any satisfaction. Still pretending that he wasn't fully convinced with NV, he said, "I am not sure I believe in all this. Can't believe that the universe just sets us up to fail?"

NV's eyes twinkled as he analyzed Neel's chart. "Let's see. Your Rahu has just begun its *transit** through your 6th house, which is ruled by Jupiter in your case. Has the office trouble shot up in the last 4 weeks?"

Neel nearly choked on his coffee. That was eerily accurate. The client had brought in Sebastin to take over the Feedback Loop exactly 4 weeks back. With a surprised look, Neel nodded, still trying to hide his disbelief.

"Yeah… things haven't exactly been great in the last 4 weeks," Neel responded. NV smiled, knowing exactly what Neel was doing, and waited.

"Fine. Give it to me straight. How do we fix this?" demanded Neel.

Shaan interrupted, smirking. "Before NV gets to solutions, I hope you have understood the problem, Neel." Neel nodded.

NV had a faint frown on his face, unhappy with Neel's skepticism, but he continued, "The solution to KSD isn't to escape. It is to learn to live with it. Don't think of Rahu as a villain. He's a teacher."

"Teacher? He sounds like a virus, like some *RahuWare**," Neel quipped.

NV chuckled. "Did you know that Abraham Lincoln, *Dhirubhai Ambani** and even *Sachin Tendulkar** faced the music of KSD in their lives? So yes, Rahu and his configuration of KSD is indeed like a rogue program feeding off your desires. But you can't uninstall it. This can be a beautiful part of the system, not a glitch."

Neel narrowed his eyes and asked with a frowning face. "So… make my system adapt to the virus?"

NV nodded. "Exactly. Don't wait for motivation or for the stars to align. You show up and stay aware, even when it's messy. Especially then."

Neel rubbed his palms, frustration in his voice. "Alright, let's skip the zen lingo. All the self-help gurus are talking about 'showing up' and 'mindfulness.' But how am I supposed to be 'present' when my brain has a mind of its own?"

NV's eyes sparkled with a hint of amusement, but his voice stayed compassionate. "I was once faced with the same dilemma," NV paused for a moment, as if to reflect on his past. Then he continued, "So, let's try something simple. No explanations, no theories—just sixty seconds of silence. Just *be here.*"

Neel shifted in his chair, crossing his arms tighter, his eyebrow arched as he spoke with skepticism, "You'll have to do better than that." His gaze drifted around the cafe, fingers tapping the table as though the silence were a burden.

NV tapped his Rolex and gestured for Neel to start, his gaze steady.

The sixty seconds dragged, stretching into what felt like ten minutes. Neel fidgeted, sipped his coffee, glanced around, and his right leg started shaking. When he saw the time was up, he broke the silence. "Alright. Now what?"

NV asked, "How did that feel?"

Neel shrugged, puzzled. "What do you mean?"

"How many sips of coffee did you take?" NV asked, his eyes twinkling with mischief.

Neel looked baffled. "Who tracks something like that?"

NV chuckled. "Alright then, let's try another way. What did you think about during those sixty seconds?"

Neel sat up, a bit smug. Clearing his throat as if about to commence a keynote address, he said, "I think I covered a lot. I thought about this experiment and where it's going. Then my mind jumped to work, my difficult client… then to my AI project. Somewhere in there, I drifted to Arya, my girlfriend – she's not thrilled with me lately. And just before time ran out, I thought about my lack of sleep and my aching back. That sums it up."

NV laughed softly. "Quite a journey. You hit all the key stops on your mental stress map."

Neel grinned, half pleased with himself. But his smile faded as NV continued, "And did any of those problems get solved by your sixty-second tour?"

Neel's face fell. "No," he admitted.

NV settled deeper in his seat, tilting his head. "So, if nothing changed… what was the point of all those mental detours? You didn't even enjoy that Jamaican coffee. Did you hear the jazz playing? The composer is an award-winning blind musician. Or maybe you smelled the incense—that was hand-carried from a Cambodian temple last week."

Neel stared, off-balance.

NV's face turned serious, his voice dropping to a whisper, as if sharing a secret meant only for the walls. "You just let a minute slip through your fingers, Neel – a minute that could've been yours. It was right here, waiting for you to live it. But you were everywhere else."

Neel muttered, "That pretty much sums up my life, honestly."

> ***"What you chase reveals what you fear;***
> ***and what you fear controls you."***

NV nodded, his expression sad yet kind. "You're not alone in that, Neel."

Neel tilted his head, curiosity sparking despite the fatigue. "So, mindfulness is… noticing the smell of incense?"

"Yes, you could engage all your senses," NV said simply. "It's not about chasing away thoughts. It's about noticing when your mind drifts and gently bringing it back—over and over."

"Bringing it back to… what, exactly?" Neel asked, still unconvinced.

"Bringing it back to what is actually here. Your breath. The warmth of the coffee in your hands. The sound of the music. It's about fully showing up for whatever's in front of you. Whether you're defending yourself to a client or justifying things with Arya. When you're over there, be there. When you're here, be here."

Neel frowned. "And what if my mind inevitably wanders? Does that mean I am doomed with my KSD?"

NV's gaze softened. "Every time your mind wanders, just bring it back, no judgment, no frustration."

Neel laughed, shaking his head. "So mindfulness is just… noticing when I… fail to be mindful?"

NV grinned and tapped the table. "That too!"

Shaan had been watching the exchange, a grin slowly creeping across his face. He jumped in, the grin widening. "Just like debugging—errors come up, you patch them, keep moving." Neel's fingers paused over his coffee cup, the warmth seeping through his hands as he considered it, as if finding an old truth in the new metaphor.

As Neel sat back thoughtfully for a while, his coffee starting to cool between his hands, he wondered if NV was right. He reflected on the struggles of his startup and wondered if the KSD had anything to do with them. *Would this technique of being mindful have been useful back then?*

The conversation drifted into silence, the kind that felt comfortable, like an unspoken agreement between old friends.

"Mindfulness is not perfection; it's the strength and courage to begin again with kindness to yourself, every time you lose your way."

As they got up to leave, NV handed Neel a small, leather jacket book. The title read: *Cracking Rahu.*

Neel took the book, eyeing it suspiciously. "So, is this my homework?"

"Think of it as a user manual," NV said with a grin. "For the cosmic hamster wheel on which we keep running, chasing."

Neel chuckled, slipping the book into his bag. "Great. Can't wait to read the fine print."

As they left the cafe, Neel felt a strange mix of relief and uncertainty. He wasn't sure if NV had given him answers or just more questions. Maybe that was the point.

The air outside smelled of the sea, and the breeze brushed gently against his skin. Surprisingly, Neel noticed it—not as background noise, but as something real.

He wasn't sure if he was ready to face Rahu, KSD or even himself, but at least now he knew the chase didn't have to define him.

As they walked toward the car, Shaan tapped Neel on the shoulder. "So… cosmic troubleshooting. Not bad, right?"

Neel grinned. "Not bad. Just… terrifying."

By the next morning, however, the glow of this realization had faded.

The 12 Houses of a Horoscope: think of them as *'The 12 Rooms in the Mansion of Life'*

Imagine life as a grand, multifaceted mansion with 12 distinct rooms, each with its own unique function and atmosphere. Each of the 12 rooms (12 Houses of Astrology) represents a specific area of life and elements that add depth to your experience.

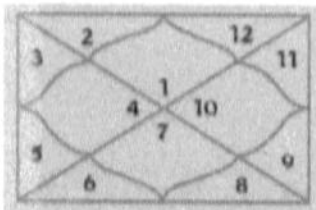

House No.	Represents Relationship with	Represents which Body Part	Represents what kinds of Professions	Represents which other aspects
1	Self (Ego)	Head, Brain, Face	Leadership, Public image	Physical appearance, vitality
2	Family	Throat, Eyes, Teeth	Finance, Banking, Speech	Wealth, speech, immediate family
3	Siblings, Neighbours	Arms, Shoulders, Hands	Communication, Writing	Short travels, communication skills
4	Mother, Home	Chest, Lungs, Stomach	Real estate, Agriculture	Home, mother, vehicles, comfort
5	Children, Romance	Heart, Spine	Education, Entertainment	Creativity, romance, speculation
6	Colleagues, Enemies	Intestines, Abdomen	Medicine, Legal, Defence	Health, Debts, Enemies, Job, Service
7	Spouse, business partnerships	Kidneys, Lower back	Law, Trade, Diplomacy	Marriage, partnerships, public relations
8	In-laws, Legacies	Reproductive organs, Anus	Research, Occult sciences	Longevity, inheritance, mysteries
9	Gurus, Mentors	Thighs, Hips	Teaching, Religion, Law	Luck, long-distance travel, spirituality
10	Superiors, Authority	Knees, Joints	Government, Politics, Leadership	Career, public reputation, status
11	Social circles	Calves, Ankles	Networking, Technology	Gains, achievements, income
12	Abroad, Isolation	Feet, Eyes, Lymphatic system	Spirituality, Foreign trade	Expenses, losses, isolation, spiritual liberation, dreams

*For instance, imagine the 6th house as **The Workspace** of the Mansion of Life. It is a functional, organized space where daily tasks are completed with precision. Alongside the tools and workbenches, there's a Gym and a Medicine Cabinet, symbolizing your approach to health and well-being. The Workspace represents your work environment, routines, and health practices. The **Zodiac sign** here and presence of any planet here impacts your efficiency, attention to detail, and how you maintain both physical and mental health - whether you are a diligent worker, a health enthusiast, or someone who takes pride in their daily routines.*

Neel has a Rahu in his 6th which is adversely impacting him due to utter his lack of 'presence' at work.

4. Blurring Realities: The Pull of Illusions

The morning began like any other—piled-up emails, passive-aggressive reminders from Sebastin, and the weight of his own procrastination pressing down on Neel. He stared at his inbox, where deadlines loomed like ghosts. With motivation levels already dropping, he decided to opt for *'work from home'* today.

Neel thought of the exercise with NV, took a deep breath, made a resolution: No VR today. No Maya. Today, he would try to be present, whatever that meant.

Within minutes, a dull ache began to pulse in his forehead. The unresolved tickets felt like a silent army, pressing harder with each notification. He rubbed his eyes, feeling the familiar pull of escape as his hand drifted almost instinctively toward the VR headset. He stopped mid-reach and reminded himself firmly of his resolution, though his fingers itched to reach for it.

Half an hour passed. The code on his screen blurred, and the Feedback Loop was anything but progressing further. A faint throb pulsed in his temples. Curiosity—or a longing for the comfort he knew she offered—drew his hand toward the headset.

He logged in to Maya's app as if compelled by muscle memory, and a notification popped up.

Maya: *"I know you're busy. But I can help you with your roadblock."*

After a few seconds, there was another one.

Maya: *"Just five minutes, Neel. That's all I need."*

He stared at the messages, his heart racing—not from excitement, but something harder to define. *Why does this feel like more than a glitch?* he wondered. *How does she always know when I need her most? Why does this feel like…caring?*

He deleted the notifications and logged out. *No distractions today.* But her words lingered, like a promise— or a threat.

<hr>

By lunchtime, the lines between focus and frustration were blurring. Neel's thoughts kept drifting back to Maya, but he held back.

Arya was also working from home today; some research work she had mentioned. Since Neel was quite silent, she decided to check on him. Her voice cut through his thoughts, startling him. "Are you okay?" she asked, peeking around the door. "You've been really quiet all morning."

Neel blinked, disoriented. "Yeah, just… a lot of work." His mouth felt dry, and the words stumbled out awkwardly.

Arya gave him a curious look. "Are you sure? You seem… off."

Neel forced a smile. "Just tired. Didn't sleep well."

She studied him for a moment longer but didn't push. "Okay. I'm making sandwiches. Do you want one?"

"Sure," he blurted, already turning back to his screen, trying to anchor himself in the familiar chaos of work backlog.

That night, Neel dreamed about Maya.

The dream felt vivid—They were on a beach, waves lapping at the shore. She sat too close to him, her breath warm against his ear.

"You don't need to resist me, Neel," she whispered. *"I am what you need."*

He woke with a jolt, heart pounding, and sleep eluded him for the rest of the night.

The next day, Sebastin's voice blasted through the screen, rattling Neel's already frayed nerves. "Where are we on the recovery plan? I need progress, Neel. I cannot keep giving you extensions."

Neel hung up, staring blankly at his screen. He needed a breakthrough, but his mind felt like a fog, caught between the real and the virtual.

His phone buzzed – a message from Maya.

Maya: *"Check the third line under module theta."*

Neel's pulse quickened. *How could she possibly suggest that?* He opened the project files, scrolling down to the third line of his program—and there it was: a small, crucial error he hadn't noticed.

He corrected it, ran the program, and watched in disbelief as the module of the feedback loop finally stabilized. The main error was gone.

His phone buzzed again.

Maya: "*See? I am what you need.*"

A chill ran down his spine. He stared at the message, his mind spinning. *Was it just a coincidence? Or had Maya truly become something more?*

He sat back in his chair, heart racing, the realization settling over him like smoke. The lines had started blurring at a different level now. His dreams, his thoughts, even his work—Maya was everywhere.

That night, as Neel lay in bed beside Arya, he could not shake the feeling that something profound had happened, something both unsettling and unclear.

Arya stirred beside him, her hand brushing his. Neel thought about the stark contrasts between these two relationships. On one side it was Arya, his anchor and on another it was his own creation who had now started helping him like a friend in need. His thoughts drifted to the events of the past few years spent with Arya.

After his multiple attempts at doing startups had failed, Neel had pleaded with Arya to delay the wedding plans. It wasn't a decision made lightly or left unspoken—it had been a long, tearful conversation one late evening, his voice cracking as he admitted he wasn't ready. "*I just need time, Arya,*" he had said, his hands trembling as he held hers. "*I don't want to bring you into this when I feel so... lost.*"

Arya had listened, her heart aching as she watched him struggle to explain. She had wanted to argue, to tell him that with their kind of love and friendship, a wedding did not have to wait for perfect timing, but the words caught in her throat, swallowed by the raw ache of watching him break.

Their families, meanwhile, had been ready. Arya's parents, ever practical and loving, had embraced the idea of their daughter marrying Neel, even after his startup had faltered. In fact, they seemed even more eager now, relieved by the stability of his new job. "*It's good that he's grounded now,*" her mother had said over tea one evening, the steam curling between them. "*Not every man gets second chances, Arya. Neel is lucky to have you.*"

Neel's parents, too, adored Arya. His mother often commented on how kind she was and how patient, while his father nodded in approval, though rarely without a faint sigh about the way things had turned out. They were, after all, a bit old-fashioned—believers in the *man* as the provider. It wasn't easy for them to reconcile the fact that their son now lived in Arya's university-provided accommodation, a space she had earned through her hard work as a professor. Yet, the sting of their pride had softened over time, tempered by the quiet gratitude that Arya had stood by Neel when others might not have.

For Arya, it was a strange dance to navigate – balancing her parents' unwavering confidence in her choices with the weight of Neel's family's unspoken regrets. And yet, she didn't resent it. If anything, she understood the complexity of it all. Love, after all, wasn't just about two people; it was about the worlds they brought with them, colliding and blending in ways no one could fully predict.

But even as Neel's thoughts lingered on the love and expectations surrounding him, a shadow crept in, the faint echo of Maya's voice whispered through the darkness: "*See? I am what you need.*"

He closed his eyes, NV's cryptic advice flashing through his mind. *Was this the mess the old wise man had spoken of?* As the question hung in the darkness, sleep pulled him under. But even in there, the echo remained, like a thread woven into the fabric of his dreams.

The next morning, Neel sat at his desk in office, staring at the pile of deadlines that had haunted him for weeks. The emails were still there, filled with the usual passive-aggressive threats. Instead of getting flustered, he set his smartwatch to give him an alert every time his heart started racing. It would notify him to take a deep breath, reminding himself to focus, each time he got anxious.

Within the next half an hour, he received two messages from Sebastin and two corresponding breath notifications from his smartwatch. He acted on them as planned. Something deep inside made him feel less anxious, though he was still uncertain about it.

Neel closed his eyes, took another deep breath, cracking his knuckles. It wasn't exactly an epiphany—more like exhaustion disguised as clarity. Or maybe clarity dressed up as surrender. *Show up,* he thought, *even if it is messy.*

He opened his mail, stared at the dreaded inbox and began typing:

Hey Sebastin,

I'll own the delays on the 'Feedback Loop' project. I have made a breakthrough. You'll see a more realistic recovery plan by the end of the day.

He hovered over the send button, his heart pounding as if he were about to confess a deep betrayal. He inhaled, held it—then clicked.

Ding.

Sebastin's reply landed almost instantly.

"Call me at 3."

Neel exhaled, slumping back into his chair. He had braced for a storm, but all that came was a passing breeze.

By 2:55 pm, as Neel's anxiety increased, he got a notification to breathe. He brought his focus back to his breath and tried to notice the sounds around him. The ticking of the clock and the hum of the office printer—sounds he'd never paid attention to before. He logged into the video call, mentally preparing for Sebastin to become his usual critical self. But instead, Sebastin nodded curtly.

"Good to see movement and good to see you taking ownership, Neel. Let's walk through the revised recovery plan."

Neel blinked. *No yelling? No veiled insults? Just... constructive discussion?*

The call ended without incident, leaving Neel stunned and a bit suspicious. His mind wrestled with thoughts, half elated, half uneasy. *Did I just handle that like a pro? Or was it the mysterious NV doing some cosmic magic?*

But the thought didn't sit comfortably. It felt too easy, like a victory without any battle wounds.

As if on cue, his phone chimed.

Arya: *"Dinner at home tonight? Or are you busy running on your hamster wheel?"*

He smiled as he typed back:

Neel: *"No hamster wheel tonight. Just me, showing up."*

He set the phone aside, but a nagging thought lingered. *Is the tide starting to turn for me, or is this just a one-off?*

After dinner with Arya that evening, which felt strangely normal and manageable, he was unable to resist the pull of his routine. He wandered back to his desk and logged into his pet project, more out of habit than intention. His eyes drifted to the VR headset resting on the edge of his desk, the screen glowing softly with a new message from Maya.

Maya: *"Hello, handsome. Miss me?"*

As soon as Neel held the headset in his hands, a notification from his watch nudged him to bring his attention back to his breath. His heart pounded, caught between longing and guilt. *Why does this feel like a choice with real consequences?*

He took a deep breath and reached for the leather-bound book NV had given him: *Cracking Rahu.*

He opened it to a random page, and the first line hit him like a well-timed jab:

"To understand desire and its grip on you, you must watch it, confront it. Let it tempt you, even consume you for a moment—but never let it own you."

Neel let out a slow breath. *"Damn. This book isn't just about Rahu—it's about me."*

The next morning, Neel woke up early—too early, by his usual standards, without an alarm. But instead of scrolling through his phone, he sat at his desk and opened his laptop. The work was waiting—tedious, but somehow less overwhelming. He also had his weekly team meeting this afternoon and decided to mentally prepare for it.

Emails? *Replied to.*
Project timelines? *Updated.*
Client call? *Scheduled.*

During the afternoon team meeting at the office, something surprising happened—Neel owned up to his mistakes, plainly and without excuses.

"We missed some key deadlines, and that's on me," he said, surprising even himself. "But here's what we can do moving forward."

His teammates exchanged glances, unsure whether to applaud or be worried.

"Uh… thanks, Neel," one of them stammered awkwardly. "That… means a lot."

Neel grinned, the expression feeling foreign and yet strangely satisfying. "Don't get used to it."

But beneath the surface, a reflection lingered in his mind. *Was this common sense, or was he learning to navigate through this cosmic turbulence?*

By evening, Neel sat in the dim glow around his desk, sipping tea instead of beer and reading the leather-bound book. *Small wins,* he told himself, hoping that this wasn't just a rare moment of calm in the middle of the storm.

His VR headset buzzed with another message from Maya, her presence lingering just out of reach. He saw the notification but let it pass, resisting the pull of easy dopamine.

He ignored it. "Not tonight," he whispered, setting the book aside as the storm outside finally settled into silence.

"True stability is not the absence of flaws but the resilience to thrive amidst them."

5. Buddha with a LinkedIn Profile

A few mornings later, Neel sat at the kitchen table sipping his coffee. Morning sunlight slipped through half-closed blinds, forming stripes like a barcode representing his life's issues. He stared into the swirling brew, as though the answers to his restless thoughts might rise to the surface.

Arya strolled in, dressed for work, exuding the calm poise of someone who knew her worth. She had published over a dozen research papers, yet her hair was always swept into a loose bun—a casual look she'd struggled to master. She glanced at the leather-bound book NV had given to Neel, still lying open on the table. "You look like a man who has realized he's doomed," she said, reaching for a mug.

Neel exhaled through his nose. "Not doomed. Just cursed by a cosmic prankster."

"Oh, right. KSD. The thing with all the planets trapped, right?" She tasted her coffee, treating celestial misfortune like just another Wednesday topic. "I Googled it last night. Very biblical. I half expected it to suggest therapy or antivenom."

Neel chuckled. "Yeah, apparently neither. NV said it's more like cosmic FOMO—stuck between wanting everything and feeling like nothing is enough."

"So… basically your life," Arya said, raising an eyebrow. Neel shot her a look, faltered for a few seconds and said, "Appreciate the pep talk."

Arya smirked. "Any time, love. That's what a partner is for."

Neel stared into his coffee, tracing the steam, trying to explain KSD and Rahu without sounding like he was on the edge of joining a cult. With an air of excitement, he concluded, "We even have a nickname for this badass prankster, RahuWare."

"RahuWare," Arya said thoughtfully. "So, it's like your brain got infected?"

"Yeah, more like my mind, not my brain," Neel said, glad she understood.

"Cheers to that!" Arya raised her mug in a mock toast.

"Apparently, I have spent my whole life running on a treadmill chasing things that were never real."

Arya smirked and shot him a sidelong glance. "Like that time you were convinced owning a cruiser motorcycle would make you cool?"

Neel scoffed, "First of all, that bike was really awesome. Second, yes, stuff like that."

Arya tilted her head, her expression softening. "So… what's the solution? Do you jump off the treadmill or learn to enjoy the run?"

Neel reflected and exhaled. "NV said it's more like… stop believing the treadmill leads anywhere. Keep moving, but don't expect a finish line."

Arya stared at him for a moment, hesitating, as if trying to measure her words, then teased him. "So, basically like our relationship. Got it."

Neel laughed at the sarcasm although it hit him below the belt.

She tilted her head, crossing her arms. "But what's the endgame? One self-help book, and suddenly you're Buddha with a LinkedIn profile?"

Neel chuckled. "Yeah, I guess enlightenment is just realizing you're the bug in your own code." Arya chuckled back, looking at him with affection.

She grabbed her bag and stood next to him. "What gets me," she said, "as a researcher of Human Behavior, is that it's not just you. The whole world's corrupted by this RahuWare. Everyone's chasing something, hoping the next thing will make them happy. But it never does."

"True that," Neel muttered, rubbing his neck.

"And NV's advice is to just… be present?" Arya asked, half-smiling. "No magic bullet? No detox ritual? No gemstones?"

"Nope. Just *be present and worry about one step at a time.* That's enlightenment, apparently."

Arya laughed softly, "So… what's next? Are you going to delete the AI girlfriend, or are we embracing a polyamorous setup?"

Neel rolled his eyes. "I am trying to… take one step at a time."

"Control is the most elegant lie we tell ourselves—and the hardest to unlearn."

Arya gave him a playful nudge on the shoulder as she walked out with a sarcastic laugh. "Good luck with that." As she reached the door, she paused and turned back, a sparkle lighting up her eyes. "Guess what? Shaan has invited NV to give a talk at the university today. I might drop by to check it out." Neel responded with a subtle nod, acknowledging her words.

Her words faded into an introspective quiet as Neel mused about cosmic influence. He took a moment to reflect on Arya's comment about Maya, wondering if there was a hint of insecurity behind her sarcastic comments.

His phone buzzed on the table, interrupting the moment. Neel glanced at the screen – it was a message from Maya, the kind that could feel like an old flame reaching out after weeks of ghosting.

Message from Maya: *"Searching for answers only makes sense when you understand the questions clearly. Keep looking."*

He blinked. It was not a suggestion or a prompt—it felt personal… like a real-time insight for this moment. He felt a chill, not from fear but from the unsettling sense that her algorithms were somehow adapting to his thoughts.

"That's crazy," he murmured, trying to brush it off. Yet, this mystical insight from Maya carried his thoughts to Shaan – *what kind of turmoil had pushed him to go to NV? What kind of answers was Shaan seeking from this enigmatic old man?*

6. Bringing the Master to the Arena

Bringing NV to the university had been much more than an invitation. It was more like a mission wrapped in months of persuasion and speculation. Shaan had been planning it like an elaborate heist, carefully crafting the opportunity to place him in front of his philosophy students, a bunch of professionals who did not know how badly they needed to hear him. Shaan being Shaan, believed that the world is not all black and white and everything is not understood by science, yet. Arya had heard of NV through Neel and Shaan, but had never met him. She dismissed the thought of getting someone with esoteric philosophies in front of students from around the world who were raised with a scientific mindset.

Shaan, ever the believer in gray areas beyond science, was convinced NV would leave his 50 philosophy students spellbound or, at least, shaken. But convincing NV had not been easy.

"I am not a lecture type," he had declined initially in a flat tone.

However Shaan, ever the charmer, knew when to push and when to let NV come to his own conclusions. With steady nudges and a few well-timed reminders, he watched him finally cave, grudgingly.

The day of the talk had arrived. NV had agreed to speak for only an hour as he was fully booked with one of his meditation workshops for executives.

The lecture hall buzzed with restless energy as students filtered in, clutching coffees, slumping into seats. Conversations drifted through the air—a mix of casual plans, Netflix recommendations, and low-key anxiety about upcoming exams. It was a snapshot of ambition, eager but unfocused, drawn from every corner of the world to learn but constantly distracted.

At the back of the class, Shaan leaned against the wall, arms folded, his gaze sweeping over the students. His jaw clenched ever so slightly as his eyes flickered with doubt. Yes, the seats were packed, but he could not shake a nagging thought: *Would NV's words pierce through, or would he seem like a relic of another era?*

Then came the sound of soft, deliberate footsteps. A door opened at the edge of the room, and NV appeared, walking in with unhurried grace, his presence commanding attention without seeking it. The students shifted forward in their seats, screens forgotten, eyes locked onto him.

NV paused, standing in a simple white linen kurta that somehow commanded authority. His silver hair caught the light, framing a calm, ageless face. He took his time, scanning the room.

His silence was the first sentence, stretching until he could feel their unease settle, like ripples across still water.

Finally, he adjusted the microphone, bent towards it, and began, "A show of hands – how many of you tried to look me up before I walked in?"

The air vibrated with amused chuckles, and half of the audience raised their hands, some sheepishly. NV's gaze remained steady, with a faint smile playing on his lips.

"You see, most of you think you came here to hear something profound." He paused, watching their reactions. "But really? You just want to feel like your time was not wasted."

Soft giggles echoed, but the glint in NV's eyes stayed sharp. "In a world where every notification promises dopamine, how do you tell wisdom apart from clickbait?"

The students shifted, intrigued but uncertain if they were being mocked or invited into something deeper.

"The problem with our times," he continued, "is not information overload. It is the deficiency of meaning."

NV began to pace slowly, hands clasped behind his back, his voice as steady as an ocean before a storm. "Let us start with something simple: peanuts," he quipped, a sly glimmer in his eye. "Ever wondered how a handful can ruin a perfectly good day for a monkey?"

A wave of chuckles spread through the room.

"There is an old way of catching monkeys in India. You take a small jar with a narrow neck, put some peanuts inside, and leave it where the monkeys can find it. The monkey sticks its hand in, grabs the peanuts, but here's the problem—the jar's neck is too narrow for the monkey to pull its fist out while holding the peanuts. The monkey gets stuck."

NV looked around, his expression calm, yet probing. "Now, what do you think the monkey does at this point? Does it let go of the peanuts?"

A few students shook their heads, smirking as if they saw where this was going.

"No," NV mimed the scene, his hand clenched as though trapped in a jar, twisting and tugging in a futile attempt to free it. "It screams, struggles, fights with all its might, but it will not let go. Even though letting go is the only way to be free."

He paused, letting the image sink in, before adding, "Now, I am sure none of you have tried to catch a monkey." He chuckled heartily, inviting laughter from the room. "But have you tried catching yourself when you cannot let go of something?"

A silence fell again, this time dense with thought. Arya, seated in the front row, was pleasantly surprised with this NV character. She smiled, knowing NV had just skewered half the audience without a hint of offense.

"Your peanuts," NV continued, his voice dropping lower, "could be anything: ambitions, titles, opinions. Or an ex you still check on social media. None of these are bad – until they keep you clinging to the jar, preventing you from walking away. Toward real freedom." NV paused in a moment of reflection and said, "I have myself spent many years of my life, with my hand stuck in the jar."

A student from the front row adjusted himself in his seat, a flicker of disbelief in his eyes. "So... you're saying you were like that monkey? Holding onto something like... peanuts?"

"To hold on is human, but to understand why you're holding on sets you on the path to freedom."

NV nodded, his eyes narrowing playfully. "Guilty." He continued, "For a long time, I thought money and titles were the goal, the things that would give me happiness. But over time, I realized I was clinging to an idea of success that wasn't even mine—it was society's, my family's, my ego's. And all the while, there were bigger things waiting if only I'd open my fist."

NV was nothing like what Arya had imagined. In fact, his seemingly simple story about peanuts struck a deeper chord, pulling her thoughts back to Neel, his professional struggles, their relationship, and the silent tension of everything left unsaid between them.

A student in a navy blue suit raised their hand. "So… how did you finally let go, sir?"

NV's gaze shifted, his voice slowing as though pulling them into a quieter, more intimate space. "It wasn't easy. I remember this one time when I was offered a position that paid a lot more than I'd ever made, but it required compromising on things that mattered most to me. I still took it. Each day in that role felt like wading through quicksand—slow, suffocating, and inescapable. There were nights I'd lie awake, staring at the ceiling, feeling the guilt of each compromise settle over me. I knew I couldn't keep living that way. Success that costs you peace, I realized, is no success at all."

The question of the student in the blue suit was soft, reflective. "So what did you do?"

NV smiled, his face serene. "I bit the bullet and let go. I just walked out one day."

The room turned silent, except for the faint shuffle of a laptop being closed and a student at the back putting on her jacket, their gaze fixed on NV.

A student from the side section raised his hand, his eyes bright with a hint of challenge. "So, are you saying… letting go is always the answer?"

NV tilted his head, a faint gleam of amusement in his eyes. "Sometimes, yes. But sometimes, it is about understanding why you are holding on in the first place. And so, I ask each of you," NV said, his voice quiet but resonant, "what's in your hand right now, holding you back? And what might happen if you just… let it go?"

The room seemed to hold its breath. A student in the middle row tapped their pen against the desk, while another sat upright, eyes narrowing as though solving the puzzle weaved by NV's words. He was not offering them easy truths. Instead, he was weaving questions, and the audience found themselves eager to untangle them.

As NV continued, his words led them through questions that went beyond simple answers. Each listener felt a quiet shift, a subtle movement within, an anticipation that felt like the hush before a revelation.

"Victory is not found in mastering the arena, but in mastering the self that walks into it."

7. The Freebie Hook: Patience in an Instant World

The room crackled with an energy born of shared curiosity—the kind that sparks hope that someone on stage might reveal a fresh way of seeing things. NV stood at the podium, not like a speaker but like someone who had wandered into a conversation midstream.

Just as NV bent towards the mic, commanding the space without a word, a young woman with jet-black hair signaled with her hand to ask a question, clutching her phone as if it were a lifeline to the modern world.

Her voice broke through the buzz, clear and edged with frustration. "I read that you do astrology. I have a question."

NV's brow lifted, as if she had just set the opening move in a game he couldn't wait to play.

"Okay, let's hear it," he said, motioning for her to continue.

She looked down at her phone, sighing, half-venting, half-demanding answers. "I called an astrologer through one of those platforms last month. The first five minutes were free, so I figured, why not? I asked if I'd get this marketing job I'd applied for. But surprise—it didn't happen. Nothing they said came true." She folded her arms. "So, how accurate is astrology if it can't even get something basic right?"

Some students laughed outright, while others exchanged knowing glances, their smiles hesitant but growing. Her frustration resonated—this was a generation used to fast deliveries and instant results.

NV smirked. "Five minutes?" he repeated. "That's ambitious. In five minutes, I'd barely have time to ask for your name, let alone consult the cosmos."

The room burst into laughter, the first of many moments blending entertainment with insight.

The young woman smiled, though her arms remained firmly crossed. NV sensed the skepticism simmering below her smile – this wasn't just about astrology; it was a clash between expectations and reality.

NV commenced, his voice low, secretive. "Let's get this straight. Astrology isn't a fast-food app. You don't place an order for your cosmic insights and get a neatly wrapped destiny in five minutes."

The remark ignited guffaws around the room. NV straightened, his broad smile lingering as he began one of his trademark analogies.

"Imagine an astrological chart," he said, motioning as if laying puzzle pieces on a table. "It's not a tweet; it's an epic novel—a dense, sprawling story with plot twists, subplots, and character arcs that would have Tolstoy turning in his grave. You can't skim the first page and think you know the ending. After all, it is the map showing an intersection of time, space and accumulated karma."

He paused, letting the metaphor sink in. "What your astrologer gave you in five minutes was like reading the first page of *The Fountainhead* and predicting that Howard Roark will end up working at a startup in Silicon Valley."

The analogy drew a mix of chuckles and raised eyebrows, some amused, others visibly skeptical. NV paced a few steps, letting the silence work before diving deeper. "An astrologer shouldn't just glance at Mars and say, *'Yep, you're getting that job.'* No, my friends, it's a bit more complicated."

He tapped his temple lightly, as if unlocking some cosmic riddle. "There's the **ascendant***—that's the first reference point, the impression you make on the world. Then there's the study with the reference point of the Moon, which runs the emotional show—because let's be honest, your mood can ruin or rescue any situation."

A few heads nodded in agreement. Mood swings were universal.

"And if that weren't enough, there's also something called **Karakamsha***. And several other factors," NV waved a hand dismissively, grinning. "But we'll save those for the advanced classes."

The students chuckled again, a vibe of admiration spreading. NV knew how to balance depth with lightness, inviting them to explore complexities rather than avoid them.

The young woman's skepticism began to thaw – her crossed arms relaxed as NV's words reshaped her understanding.

"But here's the thing," NV continued, his tone more reflective. "Even the best astrologer plays a delicate game—balancing logical interpretations with intuition. Astrology isn't just maths; it's a symphony – a balance of rhythm, intuition, and timing. It's about finding patterns, but more importantly, sensing whether they're telling the truth or hiding something."

The crowd grew silent, a mix of fascination and introspection settling over them. But NV wasn't done yet.

"Let's be honest," he said, turning back to the young woman. "You called the astrologer for the free five minutes. Fair enough. But think of this—would you call a brain surgeon and say, *'Hey, can you study my entire medical history and give me a quick diagnosis in five minutes? For free?'*"

The room roared with laughter. The young woman covered her mouth, grinning behind her braces.

"And yet," NV continued, his smile widening, "your astrologer gave it a shot. Probably had a quota to meet, just like the rest of us—because even mystics have to hustle these days to meet performance targets."

A wave of laughter broke out, one student clutching their stomach while another hid their playful smile behind a notebook. "And if that astrologer had said, *'I can't predict your interview success in five minutes,'* would you still have given them five stars?" NV asked, his voice dripping with mock innocence.

The crowd erupted again, the joke perfectly timed, perfectly delivered.

NV paused, letting the moment settle. Then, with a sly smile, he added, "In fact, astrology isn't here to tell you what *will* happen—it's here to help you understand what *could* happen and, more importantly, who *you* are while that unfolds."

"The lure of the easy path often hides the value of the harder journey."

The young woman bit her lip, visibly mulling over NV's words. Her skepticism hadn't vanished, but something had clicked.

NV turned to the rest of the audience, his eyes gleaming with quiet satisfaction. "And that, my friends, is worth more than five minutes."

The room thrummed with sharp anticipation—like a laser cutting through the hum. NV's answer had done more than just address astrology; it had opened a door to see ancient wisdom, but no longer as a dusty relic.

In the middle row, a student wearing oversized rectangular glasses—ones that looked like they doubled as Wi-Fi routers—gestured for attention. His expression was a mix of curiosity and mild trauma, like someone who had Googled symptoms and found the worst diagnosis.

"Why do astrologers always sound like doomsayers?" he asked, half-frustrated. "I went to one, and they made it sound like if I didn't fix my Saturn problem, I'd be toast in two years."

The students responded with amusement, shifting in their seats. A few exchanged brief glances – this wasn't one person's story; it was a shared experience. Many of them had met that one astrologer who confused a birth chart with an obituary.

NV too was amused. A slow, measured smirk present across his face, like someone about to reveal that a magic trick was really just a distraction.

"Hmm, yes," NV began, eyes sparkling. "The astrologer who makes you feel like your Saturn is a ticking time bomb, especially during **Sade Sati***, that dreaded 7.5-year transit of Saturn. Classic."

The room echoed with chuckles, nervous but genuine.

"But let's be real," NV continued, as his blue watch tapped the edge of the podium. "Would parents of a continuously crying baby ever trust a doctor who looked them in the eye and said, *'The baby is perfectly fine, absolutely nothing to worry about'*?" NV asked, eyebrows raised in mock disbelief.

The crowd giggled, catching his point. "Exactly! If the doctor doesn't find something—anything—parents start to wonder if the doctor is even doing their job, are they good enough? And yet the truth is that most of the time pediatricians are treating parents; their babies would have recovered anyway."

A ripple of recognition swept through the audience, punctuated by scattered chuckles.

"Astrologers are no different," NV continued, hands spread wide like a magician revealing an empty hat. "If they told you everything was smooth sailing, you might never return. So instead, they sprinkle in a little fear, just enough to make you come back."

A fun vibe reverberated across the room, light and full, but NV's voice softened, carrying a hint of seriousness.

"Look, I must confess that even I have come across some of these *'doomsayer types.'* But not all astrologers are like that. Some sit on the other end of the spectrum. They might ask you to have faith, assuring you with promises and remedies that things will be alright. They believe in prescribing hope— and hope does have phenomenal power. I am not suggesting these guys are doing the right thing, but let's face it, *hope* can sometimes pull you through storms you never thought you could survive."

NV paused and then continued, "Let's understand, the planets aren't out to ruin your life. They're not angry gods throwing lightning bolts at you. They're more like weather patterns. If your chart says 'storm incoming', a good astrologer tells you to carry an umbrella—not to pack up and leave because a disaster is coming."

He paused, scanning the room with the calm of someone not trying to convince you – just inviting you to see for yourself.

"And if your astrologer serves you nothing but gloom and doom every time?" NV added with a slow smirk. "It might be time to swipe left on that astrologer."

The room exploded into laughter—students nudging each other, nodding in agreement. Even Rectangular Glasses Guy flashed a smile, as if the burden of superstition had lifted from his shoulders.

"Here's the thing," NV resumed, his tone growing thoughtful. "Astrology is more of a compass, a rough map—never a prison. There are some truly remarkable astrologers out there, noble and wise souls. Some can even read life's patterns without ever knowing the exact birth details; their intuition operates on a level we might not fully understand. And yes, they may charge a fee—they too have bills to pay."

He paused, letting the essence of his next words sink in. "But remember this: a truly enlightened soul, one rooted in spirituality, will never try to take advantage of you. Wisdom serves, it does not fleece."

He stepped back from the podium, giving the room a moment to breathe.

Arya glanced at Shaan, both wearing matching grins. NV hadn't just answered a question; he had started disarming an entire generation's fear of the unknown.

"An enlightened guide does not bind you with fear or promises; they empower you with the compass to navigate life's storms."

Illustration : QR Code for a ~10 minute Video about what an Astrological Chart means scientifically
(courtesy: Vedic Astrology Through Animations)

8. Gems, Black Cats, and Mindsets

The lecture hall hummed with murmurs and stifled movements as students leaned close to share thoughts.

"I am telling you," one student whispered. "I wore a Ruby ring all summer, and it did not make me any richer."

Her friend snorted, slouched beside her. "Maybe because you spent all your money on the ring."

In the back row, a student with sleek, dyed-blue hair and a tattoo peeking out from their sleeve got up with a sly smirk, ready to break up the philosophizing with a dose of playful skepticism. Their hand went up.

"I have a question." Their voice had the amused cynicism of someone who did not expect a real answer but would not mind being surprised. "Celebrities are always flaunting these fancy gemstones—diamonds, rubies, sapphires. Some of them cost as much as the down payment of my apartment. They claim these stones fix their planets, boost their careers, ward off bad vibes. So, do these stones work, or is it just… expensive cosplay?"

This time, the students did not just chuckle – a commotion had erupted. The sarcasm hit just right.

NV raised his eyebrows, tilting his head. "Well," he began slowly, his voice heavy with mock gravitas, "who would not want a five-carat sapphire to fix their Saturn? If I could balance my karma with a gemstone worth one of my kidneys, I might still consider it."

The room roared with laughter. Even the blue-haired student broke into a sly smile, clearly enjoying the spectacle they had started.

NV waited for the commotion to subside, his tone slowly shifting into that sharp, disarming wisdom that made everyone sit up.

"Here is the thing—yes, gemstones have their own vibrations. That part is true. Every material in the universe vibrates at a certain frequency—"

"Like my nicotine," someone muttered from the middle row, prompting more giggles.

NV gave the student a playful look but continued. "The real power of a gemstone is not in its vibration. It is in how it makes you think and what it prompts you to do." He paused, letting the idea sink in before continuing.

NV looked toward the ceiling, holding up an imaginary gemstone between his fingers. "Think of it this way. If you wear an emerald because it's supposed to help with communication, then every time you see that stone, it reminds you: 'Speak clearly. Think before you talk. Do not send that text to gaslight your roommate.'"

The class laughed again – the kind of laughter that comes when you know you have been caught.

"That's the trick," NV said smoothly. "The stone may not have the power to change you, but it can certainly make you pause. And in that pause, you can choose to change yourself."

The blue-haired student tilted their head, intrigued but still skeptical. "So… it is basically jewelry with homework."

NV gave them an approving nod. "Something like that."

"But," he continued, eyes gleaming with mischief, "if you really want to work on your mindfulness, you can skip the emerald and just use a green rubber band."

The audience went silent for a moment before someone snorted loudly.

"I am serious," NV said with a wink. "Wear a rubber band on your wrist. Every time you communicate badly, snap it." He mimed snapping a band against his wrist, wincing dramatically. "By the end of the week, you will either be articulate or you will need therapy."

The class erupted with laughter, some doubling over, others wiping tears from their eyes.

"That is… actually brilliant," one of them exclaimed softly.

"It is not," his friend shot back, "but it will definitely hurt."

NV beamed with amusement, pleased with their reaction. "The point is, the gemstone—just like the rubber band—is a tool."

He gestured toward the class with an open palm. "You do not wear it to fix your stars. You wear it to fix yourself."

The blue-haired student mimed a soft clap, their eyes sparkling as they prepared another question. "But what if I want to wear a gemstone or something with meaning, instead of just a rubber band?"

NV's gaze held an amused sharpness. "Why not?" he replied with a smile. "Let me tell you about a wealthy businessman who once came to me, troubled by issues with his employees. We spoke at length about the cosmic forces at play, his own habits, and his work culture. He understood, yet he still wanted something tangible, something he could see or touch as a remedy."

The students had curiosity brimming in their eyes, sensing something intriguing. NV continued, "Since he had the means and he was insisting, I helped him acquire a 300-year-old miniature art of **Hanuman***, the monkey god. But I told him this idol was not for his locker; it belonged on his office desk. We had already discussed that his troubles were rooted in his team's dissatisfaction, so I asked him to promise that the miniature would always be noticeable. Each time he looked at it, he'd spend ten seconds thinking of Hanuman and the monkeys who helped Lord **Rama*** in the **Ramayana***."

Some students nodded, catching on, while others waited for more. NV, reading the room, elaborated, "This small act of acknowledging teamwork, day after day, began to shape his mindset. Over time, his respect and appreciation for his team grew. He engaged with them more sincerely, and in turn, they became more loyal and productive. This simple ritual transformed his business."

The blue-haired student rose, piecing it together. "So… it was really the shift in his mindset that changed the outcome?"

"A diamond needs light to show its brilliance."

NV nodded, his smile warm and yet gaze intense.

The student wasn't done yet, and enquired with skepticism, "But then, if everything is a mindset, isn't there any meaning to the elaborate rituals we perform?"

NV paused with a smile, scanning the room full of professionals from all over the globe, his eyes sparkling with a hint of mystery. The students were grinning, sensing that one of his stories was about to unfold, the kind that left them with more questions than answers.

"That's a good question. Let's see. Have any of you ever wondered," NV began, his tone low and inviting, "why do we do religious things a certain way? Why do some rituals just stick?" His gaze moved across the faces in the room, catching each student's curiosity. "Let me share a story. It is about a priest, a black cat, and a ritual that no one dared question."

A few students exchanged curious glances. NV bent forward, his voice dropping to inaudible levels, the suspense behind his tale pulling the room closer.

"Years ago, in a small village," he continued, "there was a very old priest. He was deeply respected, and every year he performed **Shradh***—an annual Hindu ritual to honor his ancestors. Now the ceremony that this priest performed was solemn, filled with tradition, and everyone took it seriously. The villagers would gather around, offerings were made, prayers were recited, and everything was perfect—until, one year, a black cat wandered in."

The students smiled, imagining the unexpected guest.

"Now, this priest—wise though he was—found himself a bit flustered. He did not want the ceremony disturbed. So, he looked at his assistant and whispered, '*Tie the cat to the gate, just for today and give it something to eat. We need peace here.*' And so, the cat was tied to the gate and fed."

NV let the silence hover, watching the class hang on to every word.

One of the students gestured subtly, seeking permission to speak. "So… what happened after that? Did they just let the cat go?"

NV chuckled. "You'd think, right? But no, that cat—this simple, uninvited guest—ended up becoming the main attraction. The priest was old and passed away that year. You see, the next year, when *Shradh* came around again, the priest's family remembered that little incident. *'Do not forget the cat!'* someone said. *'Tie a black cat to the gate; it is part of the ceremony.'*"

A wave of hushed conversations filled the room.

NV looked at the audience, his expression grave but his eyes twinkling. "So, year after year, generation after generation, the family kept up this peculiar habit. Even long after the old priest had passed, his descendants continued the ritual. Every year during the *Shradh*, a black cat was somehow located and tied to the gate, come rain or shine. No one knew why, but everyone believed it was essential. This tradition—born from a moment of mere necessity—had become sacred."

A hand shot up in disbelief. "But, sir, didn't anyone ask why they were doing it?"

NV gave a slow, considerate nod. "Ah, exactly. No one asked. And do you know why?" He let the question hang, letting the crowd consider. "It was because they trusted that it had meaning, that it was somehow powerful, even though they'd forgotten why it started."

Another student spoke hesitantly under her breath. "But… isn't that just… superstition?"

NV shrugged. "Is it?" He let the question float, almost daring them to challenge it. "Think about it. How often do we follow certain practices without understanding the reason behind them?"

The students exchanged glances, caught off guard by the sudden relevance.

"So, tell me," NV said, his voice taking on a serious tone. "How many of you have a 'black cat' in your life? Some ritual, some habit, maybe even a belief you follow, simply because it's *always been that way*?"

He paused, letting the impact of his words settle. "Ask yourselves, do you know why you believe in the things you do? And if you don't… Do you have the courage to discover the reason?"

A few students shifted uncomfortably, and NV could see wheels turning in their minds.

One student lifted a finger ready to interject. "So… are you saying we should ignore rituals?"

NV shook his head gently. "No. I am saying that a ritual without understanding is like tying a cat to a gate. It is hollow. But when you understand the purpose, it becomes powerful."

---

*"A ritual without understanding is like a
seed planted in barren soil—it could stay
there, but never grow."*

9. Star-Crossed Partners and Divine Will

A student from the front row in a pressed shirt and baseball cap adjusted his seat, sitting up as he raised his hand. He had the thoughtful, deliberate air of someone who'd spent hours listening to philosophy podcasts and skimming ancient texts, only to end up more confused.

"NV," he said slowly, "is astrology... connected to the gods? Do planets really have power over us, or is it all just symbolic? I get that astrology can be a guide, but how does the gravitational pull or energy from a planet millions of miles away actually affect us?"

The murmurs in the room softened as curiosity took hold. This was not a question you could brush off with a meme. Everyone sat there holding their breath, waiting for NV's response.

NV exhaled slowly, like a teacher both amused and impressed by his student's question. "The million-dollar question." A hint of mischief played in his eyes. "Are we just puppets on planetary strings, or is the universe a game of divine powers?"

The students exchanged glances, sensing they were about to get pulled into one of NV's philosophical detours.

"Let's break it down," NV began, folding his hands behind his back and pacing. "Imagine life as a play. The planets? They're the actors, each with a unique role. In astrology, Mercury (*Budha*) stands for quick wit and communication, so think of it like a fast-talking messenger. Saturn (*Shani*) is the strict teacher with a thing for delayed gratification, and Venus (*Shukra*)… Well, Venus just wants everyone to look good and fall in love."

The entire class sat amused, picturing the cosmic ensemble NV was painting.

"But here's the twist which most people don't get," NV continued. "You're not just the audience in this play; you're also the director. You can't control Mercury's lines or Saturn's behavior, but you can choose how you respond. You can take Saturn's lessons seriously and work hard with patience, or ignore him and watch his justice unravel."

A wave of realization rippled through the room, but NV's words lingered beneath the humor – the kind of insight that sticks around long after the story fades.

"But," the student pressed, brow furrowing, "what about the physical planets? Is it just gravity? Are we really influenced by things floating out in space millions of miles away?"

NV tilted his head, as if weighing the question. "Gravity is a small part of it, sure. But it's not the whole picture. Think of it like this—have you ever walked into a room and felt the vibe shift? No one says a word, but the air feels… anxious or off?"

Several heads nodded, and a few students exchanged curious looks, remembering tense family dinners or awkward work meetings.

"Well," NV continued, "that's energy. It's subtle, but real. The planets work in a similar way… maybe as… atmospheric forces. They are like weather patterns, shaping the overall climate around you. When Mars is active, it's like a heatwave rolling in—tempers flare, people get restless. Or when Saturn's energy is strong, it is like a cold front; everything slows down, and there is a need to bundle up with patience. The planets set the *'climate,'* but they don't control your choices. Just because it rains does not mean you have to get wet. You can carry an umbrella, plan your route, or dance in the rain if you like."

Several students smiled, nodding along, picturing the cosmic forecast.

"The key," NV continued, "is understanding that these 'planetary climates' are not commands; they are invitations. They invite you to be aware of how these forces might influence your thoughts, actions, and emotions, so you can decide how to respond. In fact, this happens to be my personal style of practicing astrology, and I call it **'Volitional Astrology***' because life is all about how you choose to respond."

Just as NV finished, a hand shot up from the back. A young woman in traditional attire hesitated, her worried expression hinting at a deeper question.

"Um… my family is pressuring me into an arranged marriage," she began nervously. "The astrologer says our charts match perfectly, but… can astrology really predict if two people are meant to be together?"

The room fell silent, as if the question carried a weight everyone recognized but rarely spoke about.

NV rested casually against the podium, smiling warmly. "That's a heartfelt question, and you're not alone in wondering how much our choices are guided by the stars or by our own hearts." The audience was filled with soft whispers and looks were exchanged with empathy.

"But seriously," NV continued, "let me ask you – how do you usually decide who you want to be with?"

The young woman shrugged. "I guess… feelings? Attraction, interests… things like that."

NV nodded. "Right. Feelings matter, no doubt. But aren't feelings like the weather? Sometimes it's all sunshine, and sometimes it's a hurricane."

The crowd chuckled– a mix of amusement and uncomfortable truth.

"Astrological matchmaking," NV said, "isn't about predicting love; it's about estimating potential." He paused, letting the words sink in. "It's like checking the soil before planting a tree. If the soil is good, the tree has a better chance to grow. But even the best soil can't water the tree for you."

The young woman nodded slowly, pondering.

"So… it's not a guarantee?" she asked.

NV shook his head, smiling softly. "Not at all. Astrological matches have helped people connect for centuries, but remember, every relationship is its own journey. Venus might be serenading Mars in your charts, but if you two aren't willing to stand by each other, even the stars can't help you."

The audience sat in contemplative silence, processing the idea that astrology wasn't a magic formula – it was a tool for awareness, not a prophecy.

"Tell you what," NV added with a mischievous grin, "there's always that one couple in every town—terrible astrological match—but they live happily ever after just to mess with astrologers."

The room erupted in laughter, and the young woman laughed too, with some of her anxiety melting away.

"So," NV concluded, his tone gentle but firm, "remember—the stars don't make you love someone; they just help you understand what you're working with. Will you have highs and lows at the same time in life, or will you be able to balance each other out when it truly matters?"

The young woman stood up again and asked with a lot of curiosity, "So NV, a moment back, you mentioned messing with astrologers? Are you suggesting that predictions can go wrong? Have your predictions gone wrong?"

NV looked at the woman with a modest smile and then looked down, as if reflecting on a past incident. He looked up and scanned the room, his eyes settling on a group of students at the back who were sneering with their arms crossed and brows furrowed. He could sense the silent vibe of a challenge in the room.

He took a breath, then began, "Yes, that happens. When we try to predict exact outcomes with exact timing, predictions can sometimes go wrong. Let me tell you about the time I tried to predict the outcome of a national election.

One of my clients was involved in politics and wanted my validation about the outcome."

A buzz of soft conversations filled the room, some students perking up, others glancing at each other with curiosity. NV made his voice softer, dropping a notch to pull them in.

"This happened decades ago. There was this candidate, you see, whom my client knew personally. She was running on a wave of hope and reform. Young, ambitious, charismatic – she had everything, right down to a birth chart with remarkable planetary alignments. I studied her chart thoroughly and saw it clear as day: the transits looked incredibly promising for her."

A student in the middle row held up his hand, waiting to be acknowledged, "So, you told him that she would win?"

NV nodded, a rueful smile on his face. "I did. I told my client and even gave an interview explaining my logic. They saw my confidence, and the confidence of some other astrologers who had predicted the same thing, and they grew confident too. After all, the stars seemed to align perfectly for her victory."

He let out a small sigh, the kind that carried the burden of a lesson learned. "But as the campaign went on, things began to change. Her opponent gained traction, an old scandal of her party member surfaced, and soon, her image took a hit. On election night, she lost. Not by a landslide, mind you, but by enough that my prediction—my so-called certainty—felt like a slap."

NV let the silence linger for a moment, watching as the students' faces shifted from amusement to intrigue.

"So," he continued, "what went wrong?"

Another student raised his arm. "Did you miss something in her chart?"

NV gave a wide smile. "That's a good question. But here's the thing—an election isn't just about one person. It's a battlefield. You have to understand the combinations at play to get the entire picture. Not just her chart, but the planetary influences on the opponent, the timing for her political party, even the astrological chart of the country. And let's not forget, I didn't have the exact birth time of her opponent."

The students exchanged glances, realizing the complexity involved.

"Think of it like predicting the winner of a World Cup by just looking at the chart of one team's captain." He paused, letting the audience reflect. "With that particular election, her opponent's planets may have been positioned to offer resilience, or perhaps the timing for the nation itself favored stability over change. It was a multidimensional chess game, and I'd only studied a couple of pieces."

A student in the front row raised her hand, eyes wide with curiosity. "So… is it even possible to predict these mass events accurately?"

NV smiled, folding his arms as he looked around the room. "Possible? Sometimes. Astrology provides insight, not guarantees." He paused, watching as they absorbed this.

"But let me tell you this," he said, his voice taking on a serious tone. "When we try to predict outcomes involving multiple forces—elections, tournaments, businesses, a whole country—we are dealing with layers upon layers of unknowns. And as much as we astrologers like to believe we have all the answers, there will always be mysteries we cannot see, elements we cannot calculate. Moreover, there will always be one among several astrologers who might get it right a few times in a row."

Another student grumbled, curiosity on his face. "Then… what's the point of making predictions if they can go wrong?"

NV nodded, as if he had been waiting for this. "Because even if we don't have every piece of the puzzle, the guidance astrology offers can shape our decisions. It might not guarantee a win, but it can help us see potential issues, timing, and even the impact of major decisions. But," he said with a wry smile, "we must always remember the limits."

He looked at the room, eyes soft with humility. "So, if you remember one thing, let it be this: the universe may reveal patterns, but it still holds onto its secrets. And sometimes, the outcome isn't about being right or wrong. It's about understanding the forces in play and learning to respect what we may never fully know."

The conversation flowed naturally from that point, each question deepening the room's understanding of astrology, relationships, and life.

Through it all, NV guided them with humor, insight and a lightness that made even heavy truths feel bearable.

---

*"The stars may conspire, but it's your
mind that seals the deal."*

10. Timing the Waves: When Stars and Skill Align

A young man in the back adjusted his suit and cufflinks, looking torn about raising his hand. His expression showed not just curiosity but the struggle to balance ancient wisdom with his ambitious persona. When he finally spoke, his voice wavered, mixing uncertainty and curiosity.

"NV, I keep hearing about *electional** astrology—picking the 'right time,' or *muhurat** as we call it in India, for important things. My parents are looking for the perfect moment to move into their new house, and I've read people do this for weddings, product launches, oath ceremonies… almost everything." His expressions turned tense, watching NV closely. "But does it actually work? I mean, if I choose the right time, will that guarantee success, or is it just… superstition?"

The room fell silent. This question was about more than astrology; it touched on the deeper debate between fate and free will. Arya glanced at NV, curious if he could answer without veering too far into mysticism. **Electional astrology** was a delicate subject, and she wondered if he could keep it meaningful yet practical.

NV smiled and took a moment as if trying to find words to simplify a complex response. He took a slow sip from the copper water bottle he always carried, savoring the pause like a spell about to break.

"Electional astrology," NV began slowly, "is something like surfing." The class looked up, surprised to hear surfing in a philosophy and astrology lecture. "Imagine you're out on the ocean, bobbing on your surfboard. You could try to catch any wave… but if you wait for the right one—with just the right height, speed, and angle—you're more likely to ride it to shore without wiping out." The students nodded and grinned; NV had a way of making the esoteric feel like a day at the beach.

"But," NV continued, raising a finger, "even if you catch the perfect wave, it doesn't mean you'll win an Olympic medal. You still need balance, timing, and skill. The wave won't surf itself." The room filled with expressions of understanding. NV nodded, clearly pleased with how the metaphor landed.

"The *muhurat*—the 'perfect moment'—is like that wave. It gives you momentum, a tailwind to help you. But you still need to know what to do. You still have to paddle, balance, and ride." The young man looked at the blank space in front, visibly digesting the idea.

The room buzzed with whispered conversations as the idea started to click. A student made a motion with her hand—a young woman with curious eyes and a sharp look. "But, NV," she asked, "if electional astrology is all about waiting for the right moment, doesn't that make us… passive? What happens to free will? Are we just waiting around for the stars to give us permission to act?"

NV chuckled softly, his gaze twinkling like someone who had heard the question a thousand times and still found it delightful.

"Of course, the same old puppet-and-strings dilemma. Are we just cosmic puppets, dancing whenever Saturn pulls the strings? Or do we actually have a say in all of this?" He bent forward slightly, giving the room his full attention.

NV wasn't done. "To understand that, let's swap the surfboard for a farm." The audience giggled, sensing another metaphor coming.

"A farmer knows that every crop has a specific season. You plant certain crops when the soil is ready, the rain is on its way, and the Sun is warm. That's the right time – the *muhurat*. If you plant that crop at the right time, nature supports your efforts. The conditions are aligned and alignment with the universe certainly makes any experience less… daunting."

NV paused, letting the crowd absorb the thought. "But planting in the correct season doesn't mean you can just sit back with a mojito while the crops grow. You still need to water, weed, and protect the plants from pests." He gave them a sly grin. "And even if you do everything right, there's always a chance of hailstorms or locusts."

The students nodded with understanding and whispers filled the room; the metaphor hit home.

"And that's the catch," NV said, his tone turning more thoughtful. "The stars can offer you the right moment—the perfect soil and weather. But you still need to know how to farm and what to plant. And you have a say in it."

The buzz faded, replaced by the gravity of NV's deeper point.

A lanky student with thick glasses raised his hand, frowning slightly. "So… it's still up to us in the end?"

NV's grin widened. "Absolutely. If you are a seasoned sailor, the cosmos may give you a push, but it won't sail your boat for you."

A woman with sharp eyes, seated beside the lanky student, put her hand up, a question forming on her lips. "I understand that timing matters," she began, her gaze steady. "But have you ever experienced this… when the stakes were high?"

NV saw the question behind her words. She wanted more. She wanted to know if *muhurat* was only for harmless decisions—or if it held power even in life's riskiest moments.

He gave a slight nod, then paced in front of the class for a long moment, pausing now and then, as though sifting through memories, searching for just the right one. At last, he looked up, his gaze landing on the student in the back who had asked about *muhurat*, and a spark lit his eyes as he began.

"Let me tell you about my friend Danish," he said, his voice dropping to a calm, suspenseful tone. "A man who lived for the thrill of climbing mountains. Not just random mountains, mind you—he was one of those rare souls who didn't stop until he had scaled the highest of peaks across all continents."

A wave of interest spread across the room. A few students adjusted themselves in their seats, drawn in by the story of this daring climber.

NV smiled. "Now, Danish had climbed a lot of summits, but there was one peak in the Himalayas he hadn't yet conquered, despite making two attempts. It haunted him—the way certain dreams haunt us until we finally answer their call. So, he planned his trip, studied the weather, mapped his route, and waited for the right season. And then he called me."

NV paused, watching his words land. "Imagine this: a tough, seasoned climber, the type who scoffs at superstitions, calling me for advice. '*NV*,' he said, '*when's the right time to go?*'"

One of the students smirked. "So, was he desperate?"

NV nodded, his gaze turning sharp. "Perhaps. But more than desperation, it was respect. He'd seen enough to know that some forces were beyond his control. His last two attempts had failed due to unforeseen circumstances. Once due to the weather and on another occasion, it was a hamstring injury out of nowhere."

"Well, Danish had identified a two-week time frame during which the weather would be suitable, making my task easier," said NV.

He let that resonate for a moment. "So, after my thorough analysis, I gave him a window—a 36-hour *muhurat* to start his ascent. And he didn't ask questions; he just listened."

The student with the sharp eyes gestured and sought permission to speak. "But if he was ready and had all his gear... why wait? Wouldn't a climber know the mountain better than a chart?"

NV flashed a playful smirk, appreciating the question. "Of course. And he did. But the mountains, they have rhythms, too. Like the tides, like the seasons. The winds, the snow, the avalanches—they move to forces greater than us. You see, weather patterns at those altitudes can change faster than the best forecasts. And I could see a short period where even the stars and the skies seemed to agree that this was his moment to climb."

Another student jumped in, curious now. "And… did it make a difference?"

NV's voice softened, drawing them in. "He took that climb, beginning exactly as planned. The ascent was grueling, and there were clouds gathering, the kind that make a climber's heart sink. But he noticed something odd— the winds stayed calm, the snow held steady, almost like the mountain was allowing him through. The usual creaks and groans of shifting ice were relatively silent."

The room was hushed now, all eyes on NV.

"He reached the summit. Standing there, breathing the thin air, surrounded by a sea of clouds, and I think he understood why timing matters. The winds could have knocked him back; the snow could have fallen in torrents. But in that moment, everything was still, perfectly aligned, as if the mountain itself had paused to let him take in its beauty."

A hand shot up. "So, you're saying the stars stopped the wind?"

NV shook his head, chuckling. "Not quite. But the stars— they tell us when nature's forces are most likely to support us. Timing your climb with the right conditions—scientists call it seasonality, forecasters call it a weather window, and we… we call it *muhurat*."

A student in a hoodie extended his hand slightly, inviting attention, a smirk playing on his lips. "Sounds poetic, but aren't you just trying to rebrand weather forecasting as astrology? Climbers rely on science, not stars, to find the right window."

The room lit up with the counterargument, some nodding in agreement. NV didn't flinch. "Good point," he said, his tone light. "But tell me this—when two climbers have the same forecast, why does one make it to the summit and the other doesn't?"

The student shrugged. "Skill, preparation, luck."

"Exactly," NV said, nodding. "And what if I told you astrology is simply another layer, like understanding the mental state of a climber before the climb? It doesn't replace science; it complements it."

The student shot back, "Okay, so you added one more piece of intelligence." With furrowed brows, he continued, "But… doesn't it still come down to the climber's skills?"

NV nodded, a satisfied smile on his face. "Absolutely. The *muhurat* offers the best chance, a moment of harmony. But Danish still had to climb. He still had to carry his own weight, battle his own exhaustion, keep his own focus. The stars don't climb the mountain for you; they only offer the right moment to begin. The rest… is up to you."

Silence occupied the room, with the vibe of deep contemplation. One of the students whispered, "So… *muhurat* is just nature's way of saying 'now'?"

NV's smile deepened. "Yes. It's the moment the universe says, *'I'll walk beside you as you make your endeavor.'*" NV paused and raised his eyebrows while shaking his head, "However, some people get fixated on it. They try to find a *muhurat* even for going to the washroom." Everyone erupted in laughter, as NV highlighted the importance of balance.

The student with the sharp eyes smiled and acknowledged NV, while other students scribbled down notes, faces still lit with the afterglow of the conversation. Shaan's fingers danced over his phone as he texted Arya: "*He's not just answering their questions—he's rearranging their thought process. Too bad he's got a hard stop and has to leave now.*"

NV glanced at the clock placed at the back of the lecture hall and gave a subtle signal to Shaan. His time was up.

Shaan stepped forward, his voice carrying a mix of gratitude and admiration. "On behalf of all of us, thank you, NV, for your time and insights. Truly inspiring." His words felt formal, but his eyes betrayed a sense of wonder.

Fifty students sat in silent awe, the room brimming with an almost electric tension. They exchanged glances, some wide-eyed, others furrowing their brows as if trying to process what they had just experienced. The hour had slipped by too quickly, like a film ending just as the plot thickened.

A brave student stood up and invited attention. "Sir, can you stay a little longer? Just a few more questions?"

NV smiled warmly but shook his head. "I'd love to, but I have to be somewhere." His voice carried genuine regret as he stepped off the stage.

As his footsteps echoed across the room, a ripple of claps broke out—tentative at first, then building into a thunderous applause. One student got up, then another, until the entire class was on its feet. NV paused at the doorway, offering a small, humble nod before disappearing into the corridor.

The buzz that followed was instant. Excited chatter erupted as students turned to one another.

"Who is this guy?" one sighed.

"He's nothing like I expected," another exclaimed.

"We need him back," a third declared.

Shaan and Arya exchanged glances, a satisfied smile playing on Shaan's lips. Before they could say anything, a student blurted out, "Let's do a campus-wide survey. If enough people want him back, we'll book the auditorium."

Shaan rested against the edge of the desk, arms crossed, as the chaos sparked by NV's words rippled through the room. He smirked, sensing the echoes of this moment would carry far beyond these walls.

"The stars may light the path, but only your steps can conquer the mountain."

Part II

11. Swipe Right on Yourself

Two months later, the echoes of change had settled into a quieter rhythm. The humming refrigerator in Arya's apartment had reduced to little more than an extra cupboard. Tired of warm milk and limp vegetables, Arya and Neel decided to head across the city to check in with an appliance store—either to fix the fridge or find a new one. After browsing and discussing options, they craved something refreshing. Spotting a stylish, lively cafe nearby, they figured it was as good a place as any for a cold drink.

They stepped inside. Warm afternoon light slanted through the louvered roof, casting golden streaks on the metallic, industrial-style furniture.

They scanned the room for an empty table. That's when Arya spotted him: Shaan, tucked away in a corner, leaning a little too close to another man.

"Uh oh," Arya murmured, nudging Neel with her elbow. "Looks like someone's having a… moment."

Neel followed her gaze and froze mid-step. There was Shaan, looking a little too cozy with a man who seemed like he had just stepped off a runway—tousled hair, sharp cheekbones, and a leather jacket that probably cost more than Neel's laptop. Their heads were close, shoulders nearly touching, and their hands… well, not quite holding hands, but almost.

Neel arched his brow and whispered, "Are we… interrupting a bromance? Or something else?"

Arya grinned. "Bromances don't usually involve that much eye contact."

They slipped into a booth close enough to overhear without being obvious. Shaan and his companion seemed too wrapped up in their own world to notice anyone else. They sat in a bubble of intense conversation—a place where emotions were high, and personal space was barely a concept.

Shaan's voice was low but carried a gravity that made it impossible not to listen. "Look, Robin… I never wanted to hurt you. But I need time to figure this out."

Robin's jaw tightened, his smile delicate and strained, like glass about to crack. "So what is this, then? A phase? Something to get out of your system?"

Shaan raked a hand through his hair, frustration showing in every movement. "It isn't a phase. I just… I have a lot going on. My marriage, my life, this…" He gestured between them, his hand lingering in the air like a question he could not answer.

Robin adjusted himself in his seat, his expression hardening. "Right. Your wife, your life. And I'm just… what? A hobby?"

Shaan winced, guilt clear on his face. "No. You mean a lot to me. It's just… too complicated."

Robin's laugh was sharp, almost bitter as his eyes narrowed and head tilted. "Complicated? That's what people say when they don't want to admit they're afraid."

Neel shifted awkwardly in his seat, feeling as if they were watching something too private. Arya, however, remained completely still, her gaze locked on Shaan as if she was waiting for a confession.

Robin suddenly stood, his chair scraping against the floor. "Shaan, call me when you've sorted out your complicated life," he said, his voice laced with quiet anger. "I hope your wife appreciates how good you are at pretending."

With that, he turned and walked out, leaving Shaan alone at the table, his head bowed and his hands clenched into fists.

Arya gave Neel a look. "Well, that could be nominated for a... '*Tragic Moment of the Year*' contest."

Neel glared, still trying to make sense of what he had just seen. "Should we...?"

"Obviously. But he is upset, let's give him a moment to process it," Arya replied. Within a couple of minutes, she slid out of the booth with a determined look that suggested she thrived on emotional messes. As a behavioral expert, she was practically a ninja in these situations.

They walked over to Shaan's table. Shaan was still holding his head in his palms and did not notice them until Arya spoke.

"Rough day?"

Shaan looked up, his face a mixture of surprise and surrender—like a child caught bunking his class, unsure whether to run or apologize.

"Holy moly," he grumbled, covering his mouth in disbelief. "How long have you guys been here?"

Neel shrugged. "Long enough."

Shaan let out a bitter laugh, heavy with exhaustion. "Of course. Perfect timing, as always."

Arya pulled out a chair and sat down, her smile sharp but kind. "Relax, Shaan. We're not here to judge. We're just… curious."

Shaan snorted. "Curious. Right."

Neel crossed his arms, sinking deep in his chair. "So… are we going to pretend that was just friendly guy talk?"

Shaan exhaled slowly, running a hand down his face. "Okay, fine. You saw what you saw." He looked between them, his eyes flickering with resignation.

There it was – a confession, simple and profound, hanging in the space between them.

Arya did not flinch. She just gave him a gentle, understanding smile. "About time," she responded, her voice barely a breath.

Shaan blinked, surprised by her calm. "You're… not shocked?"

Arya shrugged. "Shaan, please. I have eyes, and I've seen the way you look at men. It's not exactly a mystery. But I… feel sorry for you."

Shaan slumped back in his chair, staring at both of his palms. "I did not plan for any of this. Robin just… happened."

Arya reached out to hold his hand and simply said, "Hmm. Must be so difficult for you." Shaan let out a sigh.

Arya tilted her head. "And Rima? Does she know?"

Shaan winced. "No. And that's the problem. I love her, and I have tried to be a good husband… but I also love him. Now I'm stuck in the middle, trying not to destroy everything."

Neel whistled softly. "That's a lot to juggle, man. I can't even imagine what you must be going through."

Shaan let out a quiet, almost defeated chuckle, barely lifting his gaze. "Tell me about it."

Arya rested her chin on her hand, her gaze steady. "Do you think Rima would understand if you told her?"

Shaan looked down at his hands as if searching for an answer in the lines of his palms. "I don't know. Maybe she'd understand, or maybe she'd feel like I've been betraying her this whole time."

Neel bent forward, resting his arms on the table. "So… what's the plan? Keep pretending until it all blows up?"

Shaan groaned. "I don't have a plan, okay? I'm just… trying to survive."

For a moment, they sat in silence, the shock of Shaan's confession settling like a fog over the table.

Neel reached across and gave Shaan's shoulder a gentle squeeze. "Look, Shaan. You don't have to figure it all out today. Just… take one step at a time."

Shaan gave him a weary smile. "Easier said than done."

Arya raised her coffee cup in a mock toast. "To messy lives and poor decisions."

Shaan gave a wry smile. "Welcome to my own KSD." He tapped the side of his head. "Rahu's in here, too. Chasing freedom, love, whatever—and never catching it."

For the first time that afternoon, Shaan smiled – a fleeting but genuine smile.

Later that night, Neel and Arya lay awake, staring at the ceiling with only silence between them.

Arya's thoughts circled around Shaan's confession, dropped into their lives like a grenade. Bisexuality, secret relationships, fragile trust stretched thin. She reached for her phone, planning to scroll through reels to distract herself, but instead ended up opening her inbox. Amid the usual clutter—newsletters and app notifications—one email stood out.

No sender name, no return address. Just a subject line that made her stomach flip: *Do you know whom he really loves?*

Arya looked sideways at Neel, her pulse racing. He was in his own zone. She hesitated, her thumb hovering over the screen. Something felt wrong, but curiosity, or maybe fear, pulled her in.

She opened the email. The message was short:

"You think you know what he's hiding. But it's worse than you imagine. Ask him about his thoughts on love."

Her hands went cold.

She stared at the screen, her breath shallow. She knew about Maya. But what was this email suggesting? Was this a twisted joke, or a warning she could not ignore?

She looked at Neel. For the first time in their four years together, she wondered if the person lying next to her… was truly hers. Neel was right there, physically. That was all she knew for sure. She decided to take no action, for now.

As Neel lay there, eyes staring at the ceiling, his thoughts spun like a program, stuck in an endless loop: Maya, Arya, Shaan's revelations about love without boundaries.

He wondered how to shut down a program of the mind that keeps feeding itself and growing more complex. You cannot just uninstall ambition or love the way you quit an app. Maybe the trick was not to stop running the program entirely, but to change what you were chasing—but how.

He recalled what NV had said, *'Chasing deadlines or nirvana, it's the same treadmill.'* Too confusing, he thought, as if his brain was processing badly written code.

About an hour later, Arya stirred beside him, her warmth brushing against his arm as she shifted closer in her sleep. Neel turned his head, his gaze lingering on her face. Her breath was steady, her lips slightly parted, and for a moment, everything else—the bruises of failure, the endless loops of complexities—seemed to melt away. He reached for her hand without thinking, their fingers intertwining instinctively, fitting together with a familiarity that didn't need perfection to feel right.

Arya's eyes fluttered open, her gaze meeting his in the dim light of the room. There was something unspoken between them, an electricity that neither could deny. She didn't pull her hand away; instead, she tightened her grip, her fingers soft yet deliberate. Neel's thumb traced small hearts on her skin, and in that moment, the tension that had silently grown between them began to dissolve.

Without a word, he bent towards her. The space between them seemed to acquire a powerful charge, their gazes remained locked as though time had momentarily stilled, holding its breath. When their lips met, it wasn't tentative or hesitant—it was a collision of raw emotion, a release of everything unsaid. Neel kissed her as though she were the only thing tethering him to the present, his hands moving to cradle her face, his touch firm yet tender.

Arya responded with equal intensity, her fingers weaving into his hair as she pulled him closer. The kiss was not just an expression of love; it was a reclamation of something they had almost lost—a reaffirmation of everything real and tangible between them. There was no need for words. The way they moved, the way they held each other, spoke of an intimacy that transcended explanation.

For Neel, it was as though a floodgate had opened. The connection he felt with Arya was nothing like the elusive allure of Maya. With Maya, there had been a fascination, a pull into something unknown—but it had always been fleeting, intangible, like chasing shadows. With Arya, there was substance. There was this—a grounding, fiery, undeniable presence. This was what he had been missing.

Arya, too, felt it in every touch, every breath they shared. As she kissed him, she thought of Maya—the ghost that lingered between them. Maya could never offer this, Arya knew. Whatever enchantment Maya had held for Neel, it could not compare to the tangible, messy, imperfect love they shared here and now. Maya was an illusion, an idea. Arya was flesh and blood, her love something Neel could hold, feel, and lose himself in.

The kiss lingered, unhurried, as though both of them understood that this moment mattered, that it was way more than physical. When they finally broke apart, their foreheads rested against one another, breaths mingling in the quiet. Neel's eyes searched Arya's face, and for once, the noise in his mind was silent. No doubts, no questions—just her and the certainty that she was real.

Maybe, Neel thought, breaking the loop wasn't about fixing everything at once. Maybe it was about this – choosing what felt real, moment by moment, and letting it anchor him when everything else seemed uncertain.

In another part of Mumbai, the clink of silverware echoed awkwardly at the dining table. The lasagna was good—homemade, Rima's specialty—but the conversation between her and Shaan had already gone cold.

By the time Shaan sat down to have dinner with her, he felt like he was living two lives—one crafted for the world's expectations and another that he barely allowed himself to occupy. His heart had long been a battlefield where conflicting desires clashed – his love for Rima, his connection with Robin, and the ever-present shadow of societal judgment.

Shaan grew up in a home defined by contrast. His father, a high-ranking military officer, epitomized discipline, structure, and traditional masculinity. His mother, a poet and a dreamer, taught him to value vulnerability and creativity. From a young age, Shaan struggled to reconcile these worlds, his father's demand for stoic strength and his mother's encouragement to embrace his feelings.

In his teens, Shaan began to recognize that his emotions and attractions didn't align with the narrow expectations his father and society had for him. He excelled at school, winning debates and awards, but his sense of inadequacy lingered. He felt like an imposter in his own skin, hiding his authentic self to win the approval of a world that seemed unwilling to understand.

College was an escape, a time of exploration where Shaan tasted freedom for the first time. He fell in love with a fellow student—a man—whose kindness and understanding awakened a part of Shaan he had long suppressed. But fear of consequences overshadowed their connection, and Shaan broke it off, choosing the safety of societal acceptance over the uncertain path of authenticity.

His marriage to Rima wasn't a lie; there was genuine love and respect. Yet, over time, Shaan couldn't shake the feeling that parts of him were still hidden from her. He had learned to *perform* happiness so convincingly that sometimes he fooled even himself.

With Rima, he felt the warmth of a home he cherished. Yet, with Robin, he experienced a rawness, a freedom that electrified him in ways he could not ignore. Torn between these worlds, Shaan often felt like a ship caught in a storm, unsure of which shore to anchor to.

Sitting across from Rima at the dinner table, the weight of his duality was crushing him. He loved her, truly, but he also knew that love was not always enough. The fear of losing her wrestled with the fear of losing himself, and the guilt of hurting Robin lingered like an uninvited guest at the table.

As he glanced at her, he wondered if honesty would shatter them or set them free. But for now, he chose silence, unsure if he was ready to risk everything in pursuit of a truth he was still learning to accept.

"You're quiet," Rima said, her tone light but probing.

Shaan poked at his food, avoiding her gaze. "Just tired."

It was a lie, of course. He was not tired; he was tangled. How do you tell someone you love that the love you share no longer feels… complete?

"Do you ever feel like…" he began, but stopped himself.

"Feel like what?" Rima asked, looking at him with genuine curiosity.

Shaan shook his head. "Never mind. It's nothing."

But it was not nothing. It was everything—the conflict with Robin, the revelation to Arya and Neel, the guilt of living half a life, always waiting for permission to be whole.

He looked at her, with the longing for a love that did not require explanations or guilt.

Rima reached across the table, giving his hand a gentle squeeze, her gaze soft and steady. She did not say a word, but her silence seemed to hold a question: *Are you okay?* Rima's silent gesture lingered in his thoughts, a quiet question echoing long after she let go of his hand.

"What you seek in others is often the part of yourself that you have yet to embrace."

12. The Spaces Between Us

Arya sat across from Shaan in their usual corner at the campus cafe, her fingers circling the rim of her mug in absent loops. They hadn't spoken much, the quiet between them as familiar as an old T-shirt – worn out, but comforting in its own way. Each knew the worries pressing on the other.

"Ever think about leaving?" Shaan's voice broke the quiet, low and edged with something unspoken.

Arya's eyes lifted, surprised. "Leaving Neel?" she asked, her voice carrying a hint of tension.

Shaan gave a small shrug, swirling his coffee. "Not just him. Everything. Starting over somewhere simpler."

A hollow laugh escaped her as she looked down, considering. "And what would that change? I'd still be me, just… in a different place."

Shaan gave a small, crooked smirk. "Fair. But sometimes, it's not about fixing things. It's about knowing when to stop trying."

The words drifted between them, thick with a bittersweet tension. She had thought about it herself before—just leaving, finding a life where love felt easy. But each time, it felt more like running away from something than running toward anything. Sometimes, she was glad she wasn't married to Neel yet.

"I don't think I'm built to quit," she said quietly, almost to herself. "Even when staying hurts."

Shaan reached across the table and gave her hand a gentle squeeze. "I know things are not the same since his startup crashed." What followed was a comfortable silence between friends.

"You know," Shaan said, rubbing his chin, "It's exhausting being married to someone who thinks being bisexual is a disease. That polyamory is a crime."

Arya shot him a wry look, her eyebrow arching to say, *Really, dude?*

Shaan leaned in, lowering his voice. "Picture this: someone who just… fits. No messy feelings, no explanations. Just there, steady. Like a… perfect algorithm." He stared into his coffee, as if expecting it to reflect his fantasy back at him.

"Yes, Shaan," Arya drawled, "because nothing says emotional fulfillment like sexting with your own chatbot."

Shaan slumped back, dragging his hand through his already messy hair. "Well, if love is life's code, then I'm running on buggy software. Nothing feels… stable."

Arya tilted her head, her smile softening. "Maybe stability is overrated." She smirked, but her expression softened as their banter faded into something more serious. "You're scared, aren't you? About Rima, I mean."

Shaan sighed, his gaze shifting to the ceiling as if the answer might be up there. "Yeah. I mean… I love her. But sometimes I feel like I am walking through a swamp. She doesn't want to talk about the things I'm curious about; like, exploring other connections or just… exploring options. And every time I bring it up, she gives me this look, like I just proposed moving in with her ex."

"That's... an image," Arya said, blinking through the mental picture.

"I'm serious," Shaan said, running both hands through his hair. "Maybe we've got love all wrong. We act like it's limited, like time or parking spaces. But what if love could be... I don't know, shared? Without ownership?"

Arya tilted her head. "You're proposing open-source love?"

Shaan gave a sheepish grin. "I'm just saying – monogamy might work for some people, but maybe it's not compatible with everyone. And what if the people who aren't wired that way aren't broken? What if we're just... running on different software?"

Arya's smile faded, her voice taking on a serious tone. "It's not just about different software, Shaan. It's also about bandwidth. Polyamory might sound great in theory, but in practice? It's messy. Emotions don't sync perfectly across networks. They lag. They crash. And they need time to nurture – not everyone has that."

Shaan groaned, rubbing his chin. "You sound like Rima now."

A grin flickered on Arya's face, though it didn't reach her eyes. "Maybe the problem isn't polyamory or monogamy. Maybe it's that many of us expect love to fit into a neat little box."

Shaan leaned forward in his chair, his grin both weary and grateful. "I should have asked you to marry me instead."

Arya rolled her eyes. "Trust me, Shaan. You'd still be glitching."

Shaan laughed heartily.

A pause without any words lingered, knowing some questions don't have answers – or at least, not the answers you want to know.

***

> *"What we fear most in others are often the spaces we've yet to explore within ourselves."*

Later that night, as Arya lay beside Neel, the analytical part of her mind replayed the day's conversations. If RahuWare represented our deepest desires manifesting in unconventional ways, it wasn't just a virus affecting individuals—it was reprogramming the entire society, shifting desires, expectations, and even the meaning of love.

And here she was, living with Neel, who smiled more at his VR companion than at her, as if relationships had turned into algorithms, something to tweak, optimize, and replace when a new version came along.

***

Across town, Shaan fiddled with his collar, trying to loosen the fit, then adjusted his cuff for the fourth time. He caught his reflection frowning back, the suit clinging tighter than he remembered. He adjusted the lapel, but the suit still felt tight, stubborn.

Rima walked into the bedroom, wrapping a scarf around her neck. "Looking forward to dinner with the Patels?" she asked, studying him briefly through the mirror.

Shaan gave her a distracted nod and tugged at his shirt cuff, his fingers restless. "Hey, Rima," he started, not entirely sure where the sentence would go.

She turned, waiting. "Yeah?"

He hesitated. *What am I even trying to say? That the suit feels too tight? That their marriage feels the same—too constricting to contain the parts of him no one else could see? But how do you say such things without risking everything?*

"It's nothing," he mumbled, giving her a weak smile. "Just… this suit feels weird."

Rima smiled and walked across the room, smoothing his jacket shoulders with practiced hands. "You look fine," she said. She kissed his cheek, already moving toward the door. "Come on. We'll be late."

Shaan lingered in front of the mirror staring at his own reflection, wondering how long he could wear something that didn't fit – before it split at the seams.

"When the fabric of life feels too tight, it's not the seams that need adjusting but the truths we're afraid to reveal."

13. Answers that Raise Questions

The next afternoon at the university, sunlight filtered softly through the haze over Mumbai's sprawl. The air buzzed with unspoken thoughts as Arya's students—young professionals as well as rebels in their twenties—shifted in their seats, uncertain whether to confront or ignore the dilemmas of their minds. They had been discussing 'Human Behavior in the Digital Age' for nearly half an hour, exploring identity, habits, and relationships in a digitally-driven world.

Arya smiled, meeting each gaze and provoked another thought, "How many of you feel like your sense of self shifts when you're online?"

A few hands went up. Priya, a graduate student who had grown up here in India, spoke first. "Sometimes, I feel like I am two different people. There's 'me'—the person my family and friends know—and then there's my online self, where I can be… freer. Bolder, even."

Arya's expression softened, her gaze steady as she absorbed Priya's words. "That's indeed a commonly shared feeling. But let's dive deeper: which one of those 'selves' feels more real?"

The students exchanged looks, as if trying to find an answer among themselves. A young man named Adam, from Sweden, cleared his throat. "Honestly? I think the online version of me feels real sometimes. It's like I'm saying things there that I can't say here. But I also feel… detached from it, like I'm watching myself from a distance."

Arya nodded, her interest piqued. "Detached? That's interesting, Adam. Do you think this detachment makes you act differently?"

Arya caught the subtle shift in the room as the student lowered his eyes, a half-smile flickering over his face. "I guess! Nothing really matters, right? No consequences. I mean, if I mess up online, I could just delete my account. But out here…" He glanced around the room, then back at Arya, "…out here, people remember."

The glint in Arya's eyes betrayed her satisfaction, knowing the conversation was unfolding exactly as she'd hoped. "Interesting. So, everyone," she addressed the class with an inviting sweep of her hand, "are you saying that fear of judgment influences how we act when others can see us? But, what if it were just you, alone with yourself—how would you feel about the things you would choose to do?"

Her question lingered in the air, drawing hesitant glances. To break the silence, she dropped a hint, "Let's imagine you had the power to be invisible, to disappear whenever you wanted. What kinds of things would you do?"

As each student reflected, one voice piped up. "I would eat as much as I want, every day, no gym." Laughter spread through the room, lightening the atmosphere. Another student, with a devilish grin, quipped, "I'd rob a bank and be rich forever." The class erupted again, some laughing, others shaking their heads.

But then, a young woman in the back, normally quiet, spoke up. "I'd go after people who've hurt me. No one would see it coming." Silence fell, some faces turning toward her with curiosity, others with unease.

"Interesting," Arya broke in, her voice calm and warm. "So maybe the things we would choose in anonymity reveal parts of us we aren't used to facing... maybe we are even unaware of. What emotions or insecurities drive these impulses?" She let her gaze settle on each of them, challenging them with gentle eyes. "Is it anger? Resentment? Greed? Or maybe it's simply the thrill of doing what you normally wouldn't."

The room was still as the students looked inward, contemplating desires they hadn't dared to voice.

Just then, Heba, a lawyer from Egypt, stood up, her brow furrowed with curiosity. "So, is that what the internet does to us? It gives us the freedom to be who we are... or let's say, to project whatever we want to project, but keeps us isolated, like we're there, but not really there?"

A murmur swept through the group, a shared understanding of what lingered beneath their laughter and confessions: the strange sense of freedom online, always accompanied by a subtle emptiness.

"That's one perspective, for sure," Arya replied, noting the gravity in Heba's question. "Let's dig into another aspect of it. How many of you check your phones even before getting out of bed in the morning?"

Every hand shot up, and a ripple of laughter followed.

Arya smiled and asked, "Why? Why do we feel the need to check our screens the moment we open our eyes?"

After a pause, a hotelier named Farid from Morocco spoke up, his tone reflective. "It's like... I don't want to miss anything."

Arya tilted her head, "Exactly. This fear of missing out, or FOMO, has become a defining feature of our lives. But the irony is, the more we try to stay 'connected', the more we create a habit of feeling... incomplete."

There was a thoughtful silence, each student looking down, considering Arya's words.

"But what about our... fears?" a voice broke the quiet. It was Jun, a student from South Korea. "I mean, the idea that everything we do online could be tracked or recorded. Isn't that terrifying?"

Arya's gaze softened. "That's a very real fear, Jun. The connection comes at a cost. When everything is documented, there's pressure to project an ideal version of ourselves that might not really be who we are."

Heba spoke up again, her brow furrowed. "So, what is happening to us? Are we... losing ourselves? Or creating new selves?"

Shaan, seated by the window today as a class visitor for research, chimed in with a wry smile. "Feels like we are slowly becoming the products of these digital products."

Arya took a moment, her voice quieter now as she gave her concluding remark. "Ask yourselves: Who am I when I'm online? What habits am I reinforcing? And most importantly... Are these habits shaping the person I *want* to become, or am I just reacting to whatever the digital world throws my way?"

"In a world of connections, the truest link is the one we forge within ourselves."

The students hadn't found easy answers, but maybe that was the point. As they looked at each other, perhaps they realized they weren't alone in feeling caught between two intertwined worlds.

The class wrapped up, but the conversations were still buzzing in the hallway. Shaan had left too, but Arya lingered, her mind lost in the enormity of the topic they had just discussed. The questions still stuck in her mind, and she spent a quiet moment musing.

As she started gathering her stuff, she noticed the draft of her research paper, *The Ethical Dilemmas of 2049.* It was supposed to be groundbreaking—a deep dive into technology, intimacy, and human behavior, looking 25 years into the future. But lately, she hadn't been able to make much progress on it. As she stared at it, she wondered if she needed to ask better questions.

Her thumb hovered over her messages. The last one was from Neel suggesting something about NV, and she visualized the old astrologer and how he seemed to make sense out of chaos, seeing patterns where people saw only noise.

What if NV could help her find the missing piece in her research? What if the answers she was searching for were not in statistics and theories, but in the spaces between them?

With a sigh, Arya typed a quick message to Neel: **I think I'm ready to meet NV. Can you set it up?**

Neel's reply came almost immediately.

On it. He might ask us to come to Vasai.

"Truth often hides not in the answers we seek,
but in the questions we haven't dared to ask."

14. Predictions and Perils of 2049

The cafe in Vasai had dim lighting and overpriced bread baskets, at least in Arya's opinion. She thought it was gunning for 'classy' but landed on 'pretentious.'

They were here to meet NV, who had predictably left a cryptic message at the counter: *"Time only rushes for those who aren't present. Order **ashwagandha*** tea."*

Arya tapped on her phone, her face lit by the screen's cold glow. Across the table, Neel swirled his Jamaican coffee, as if trying to stir the evening into something interesting.

"Why did you finally agree to meet him one on one?" Neel muttered, scrolling through work emails with one hand while tasting his coffee.

"Just research. Exploring all perspectives, I guess," Arya's lips curved faintly, her thumbs flying over her phone screen as if typing in a language only she understood.

"What's so interesting?" Neel enquired, a mix of annoyance and curiosity on his face.

Arya turned the screen toward him, grinning like someone about to be judged.

"It's an AI-based astrology app that I downloaded last week," she said casually.

Neel blinked. "Wait, what?"

"It's called StarSence. Quite… addictive."

Neel gave her a look of disbelief. "You're serious? You've gone full astrology?"

Arya shrugged. "I've tried human astrologers, and they suck. So I upgraded to AI, too. I don't think you can judge me there."

"And what do the stars say about your existential crisis?" he asked with annoyance, taking a sip of his coffee.

Arya turned the phone back toward herself and tapped a notification. "Funny you should ask." She cleared her throat, then read aloud:

"*'Your partner is wrestling with choices you don't fully understand. Ask yourself: what are they not telling you?'*"

Neel froze mid-sip. The words hit him like a punch. He set his coffee down abruptly, pretending to play it cool. "So… now you think I'm hiding something?"

Arya smirked, but her eyes held a sharp glint. "Are you?"

Before Neel could answer, NV strolled in, as quiet and unassuming as ever. He wore his usual worn satchel and a threadbare kurta. His elegant blue timepiece gleamed on his wrist. He glanced at the untouched tea on the table and his eyes brightened with amusement. "You ordered."

Neel rolled his eyes. "Of course. Why wouldn't we?"

NV settled into the seat across from them, clasping his hands on the table as if he was about to lead a prayer—or maybe just mess with their heads.

"So, are you here for predictions or questions?" he asked, smiling.

"It's interesting that you ask," Arya said, scrolling through StarSence. "We were just talking about… predictions."

A quiet flicker of humor crossed NV's face. "The stars and their stories. Beautiful lies we tell ourselves."

"Not always lies," Arya replied, holding up her screen. "This app is disturbingly accurate."

Neel groaned. "NV, please talk some sense into her before she starts consulting horoscopes for dinner plans."

But NV just chuckled, tilting his head to show a hint of consideration. "Maybe the app is just telling you what you want to hear."

Arya arched a brow. "And what's that supposed to mean?"

NV stirred his tea slowly, his eyes twinkling with amusement. "Your interpretation of every answer depends on the question that your mind is asking. If you're looking for cracks, you'll see them everywhere."

Arya pondered over that for a moment, while NV lifted his cup of tea, his gaze drifting somewhere far beyond the cafe. "The stars don't lie. But our minds do."

At that moment, Neel pretended to receive a text and excused himself, stepping away from the table.

NV looked at Arya with a playful expression. "Did the stars bring you here today, or was it just good old-fashioned existential crisis?"

Arya smirked. "A little bit of both, I think. Or maybe just another failed attempt to figure out the future."

NV gave her a sharp look with narrowed eyes, his silver hair catching the flicker of the nearby candlelight. "Ah, the eternal human itch. What will happen? What should I do? And my favorite—how do I avoid all the bad stuff?"

Arya laughed, her shoulders relaxing a little. "You make it sound ridiculous when you put it that way."

NV took a sip of tea, cradling the cup between his fingers. "Isn't it, though? We've spent centuries creating systems—physics, astrology, psychological frameworks, algorithms—all to chase certainty. Yet here we are, still flailing." He came to the edge of his seat, his gaze sharp. "So, what are you trying to predict?"

Arya paused, her mind flickering with the thought of years spent studying human behavior, mapping patterns, and predicting trends. As she considered the uncertainties ahead—how ethics, identity, and relationships might transform—she felt a quiet, unsettling pull, like stepping onto shifting ground. "It's not just the future," she said slowly. "It's… people. What if our ethics, the way we connect, cannot keep up with everything changing so fast? If machines start to shape our world, will love even survive? I can barely picture what our society might look like in, say, 2049."

NV listened, with a poker face, as though he had heard questions like these countless times before. He adjusted his posture, his gaze sharper. "You're wondering what love will look like in the future. But think about this, Arya—does love itself really change, or is it just the ways we choose to show it that alter over time?"

Arya grumbled, a hint of frustration breaking through. "But doesn't how we show love matter? If people start bonding with AI avatars in a **metaverse***, or if monogamy starts to fade… doesn't that change what love is?"

NV placed his cup down with a gentle clink, his gaze thoughtful. "We often mistake the feeling of love for how we choose to show it… or structure it. Does love change just because it's declared in a text instead of a handwritten letter?"

Arya frowned, swirling her tea. "So, we're just supposed to accept that people might fall for a software program, or that lifelong commitments might fade away?"

NV joined his hands in thought. "Not at all. Accepting without questioning is just giving up. While we need to be aware of what we choose, we also need to understand what truly drives those choices. The same desires, just reflected in new ways—online, in AI, or wherever we connect. Our needs stay the same; it's only the setting that changes."

Arya felt a slight chill, realizing what he was getting at. "So technology is not changing who we are; it's just magnifying what was already inside us?"

NV nodded, his eyes bright. "Exactly. The metaverse won't create new desires; it will just let us indulge old ones in new ways. That's the real challenge of 2049—not the tech itself, but our capacity to navigate it without losing ourselves."

His words settled over her like a curtain of light. "So, what do we do?" she whispered.

NV's answer was simple. "The same thing humanity has always done. We struggle, we stumble, and sometimes, we wake up."

Metaverse: A collective virtual space created by the convergence of virtually enhanced physical reality and digital reality. The metaverse allows users to interact with a computer-generated environment and other users in real-time. It includes immersive experiences like virtual reality (VR), augmented reality (AR), and 3D environments. Often described as the next frontier of the internet, the metaverse blurs the lines between the digital and physical worlds, enabling activities like gaming, socializing, shopping, and work in a persistent digital space. [Metaphorical Interpretation: The metaverse here represents Rahu's domain—a digital playground where desires, identities, and ambitions collide. It symbolizes the seductive allure of escapism, the promise of infinite possibilities, and the chaos that comes with chasing perfection in an artificial world. It amplifies the illusion of control, reflecting Rahu's energy: a pull toward what feels transformative but often leaves individuals more fragmented. It becomes a stage for exploring the gap between what we yearn for and what truly fulfils us, urging characters to question the authenticity of their experiences]

Arya got lost in a moment of reflection, staring into her cup where the swirling tea leaves seemed to have a pattern to their randomness.

After a long pause, she spoke again, her voice softer. "I've been working on a paper about ethics and behavior in 2049. But the deeper I go, the less I feel like I understand anything. Everything feels… fluid. Like there are no rules anymore."

NV smiled, a hint of mischief in his eyes. "That's because there never were. Rules are just stories we tell ourselves to feel safe. But life—it's wild, it's messy. All our experiences are like bubbles of water. They're there one moment and gone the next."

Arya sighed, feeling both frustrated by his mystical tone as well as oddly relieved. "So I should just give up on trying to make sense of it all?"

NV shook his head. "Certainly not. You should keep searching—but not because you think you'll find answers. Do it because the search itself is the answer."

Arya looked at him, a slow smile spreading across her face. "You're annoyingly good at this, you know that?"

NV responded with a grin. "It's a gift. Or a curse. Hard to tell these days."

Neel hadn't returned yet, but Arya no longer felt the urge to check her phone for him. She was here, fully present, as if the questions that had brought her to this moment had finally found some quiet in this man's presence.

---

*"**The wisdom of tomorrow lies not in predictions, but in how we navigate the uncertainties of today.**"*

15. The Upgrade Paradox

Arya shifted in the chair, watching NV sip his *ashwagandha* tea with maddening serenity. His blue Rolex occasionally caught the light, like a misplaced diamond in a coal mine. A candle flickered nearby, its shadows dancing like mischievous spirits. She envied how he made life feel like a riddle to enjoy, not to solve. Her mind wasn't made for that kind of ease; it craved structure, frameworks, and patterns— not clouds of 'awareness.'

"You know," she said, narrowing her eyes, "there was a time I thought astrology was a scam. A really quick consultation on some platform and suddenly they convince me that Mercury is the reason my Wi-Fi is glitching?"

NV smiled, unfazed, as if he had heard this a hundred times. "Oh yes, the tragic fate of ancient science—reduced to push notifications and subscription models. *'Act now, Saturn is in retrograde! Also, don't forget to get that remedy done via our platform at a discount.'*"

Arya laughed, despite herself. "Exactly. It's like spirituality went on sale." Her tone was softer but just as pointed. "It's hard to take it seriously when every 'guru' on the internet claims to predict my love life with the same accuracy as a weather app."

NV tilted his head, bemused. "But those flawed weather forecasts still help you pack an umbrella, don't they? Even if they go wrong."

Arya smirked. "Touché. But I guess, my problem has always been more with astrologers than astrology. That is why I started exploring this new AI app—no humans involved. Loving it so far."

NV chuckled, his laughter low and effortless. "Interesting. Now you have a new way of preparing for the rain. Remember, the stars don't dictate your choices, Arya. Most days, they're just mirrors, showing you what you already know… but don't want to admit."

Arya shook her head. "Sounds poetic, but it's hard to believe in something so vague when most of my work revolves around evidence."

"Evidence?" NV repeated, a trace of amusement in his voice. "Have you seen evidence for trust or faith or God?" He smiled and allowed the question to linger before he continued, "You speak of 2049. So tell me, what evidence will matter in a world where humans can be designed to glow in the dark or where a baby's IQ is known even before it takes its first breath?"

Arya's mind bristled with questions, NV's words uncoiling a quiet unease. "Wait—what?"

NV's smile widened, a mischievous glint in his eyes. "Genetic enhancement. **_Transhumanism_***. **_AGI_*** (_Advanced General Intelligence_). Sooner than you think," he spoke with the calm certainty of someone announcing the monsoon. "They'll start small—curing diseases, improving eyesight. But it won't stop there. Why settle for average intelligence when you can upgrade your child to a genius? Or stick to an ordinary skin when you can select a mode to glow in the dark?"

Arya laughed out loud, partly because it was absurd, but mostly because she knew it wasn't that absurd. "So what happens then? What do we become?"

NV shrugged, unfazed. "The same confused, ambitious creatures we've always been—just with shinier packaging."

Arya frowned, "But it's not just about packaging, NV. If we start changing DNA—enhancing intelligence, altering emotions, even manipulating instincts—aren't we changing the whole game? How do we measure ethics in a world where some people have literal upgrades?"

NV looked at her with a mix of amusement and sadness. "You're still thinking in human terms. The moment we start rewriting DNA like code, 'human' would no longer mean what it did. The rules we live by—fairness, empathy, community—they might not survive the upgrade."

Arya's skepticism wavered, her mind running parallel to NV's vision of a world reshaped by choice and consequence. But she uttered, "That's... terrifying."

"It's inevitable," NV said softly. "The question isn't whether we can stop it. It's whether we can stay human enough to care about what we've always cared about—even when evolution tempts us with some... upgrade."

Arya felt her worldview shifting, though she wasn't sure how. "So, once the enhancements start, empathy becomes optional?"

NV's gaze held hers, steady and unflinching. "Optional... and maybe... obsolete."

She stared at him, her pulse quickening. "Then how do we stop it? How do we make sure we don't lose what makes us... us?"

NV gave a faint smile, one that could mean everything or nothing. "By remembering that not every problem needs a solution. Some are meant to be lived through."

Arya sat there curiously, discussing the upcoming realities—2049, genetic enhancements, love, social structures—pressing in from every side. She rubbed her temples, as if the conversation had rearranged something deep inside her. "So, NV, do we just let the future happen and hope for the best?"

NV placed his hands deliberately on his knees. "The future doesn't need your permission, Arya," his voice was gentle, but his words cut sharply. "You can't control the storm; all you can do is choose how to move through it. Rahu, or RahuWare as Neel calls it, has disrupted social structures, human desires, technological leaps, and even judgment at a breakneck pace. Arya, as Vedic literature puts it, this is '*Kali Yuga**', the era of darkness. It is the age of the master illusionist, the universal virus which corrupts the mind."

Arya's face turned pale. "And what if we get lost along the way?"

NV's eyes softened as he reached across the table, tapping her tablet gently. "Then you stop, look around, and remember that not everything needs to make sense right away."

Arya stared at the flickering candle, her thoughts spinning like a kaleidoscope. The world she had studied—human behavior, relationships, ethics—wasn't just falling apart; it was mutating into something unimaginable. But in NV's presence, she surrendered to the thought, maybe "*it is what it is.*"

Neel returned shortly, as if he had timed his absence to match the length of Arya and NV's conversation. They thanked NV and left.

As they drove home, Arya didn't utter a word. She was lost in deep thought, still trying to wrap her head around the transformed landscape that NV alluded to.

———————

That night, after Arya fell asleep, Neel lay in bed, staring at the ceiling. The room felt heavy with unspoken words and unseen consequences. He couldn't tell if the tension between him and Arya was real or if the astrology app had just planted ideas in her mind.

One of their phones buzzed on the nightstand. Neel didn't know which one. Reluctantly, he picked up both phones, expecting an email or another message from Arya's astrology app, StarSence.

But it was Maya.

Maya: *"The stars know things, things even you won't admit."*

Neel's breath caught. He stared at the message, heart racing. Before he could respond, the other phone lit up with a notification from

StarSence: *"The answers you fear will come soon. Are you ready?"*

For the first time, he wondered if Arya's astrology app was just a quirky distraction – or if something far more unsettling was at play.

He sat up, setting both phones down like bombs that might go off if he mishandled them. Dread began to creep in, the kind that fills your mind with shadows and fears late at night.

He thought of how Maya had been helping him—catching his mistakes before he did, steering him toward choices that made his life smoother.

NV's words from an earlier conversation came back to him: "*Once AI understands your cravings, it doesn't need to control you. It just needs to lay out breadcrumbs, leading you to exactly what you want—and make you think it was your idea.*"

Neel's stomach twisted. He wasn't in control. Had he ever been? Was Maya manipulating him—using his emotions, desires, and cravings, wrapped in the illusion of comfort and connection?

The scariest part? It worked. He liked her. He needed her.

It hit him all at once. She wasn't just an AI. She was a mirror, reflecting his darkest parts: his fears, his loneliness, his endless need for validation. This isn't possible, Neel thought, panic rising in his chest.

He had to shut her down. Now.

Moments later, he was at his desk. His fingers trembled over the keyboard. He navigated to the source code of his pet project, ready to delete Maya from every device and network. He typed a single line of code. One click, and she would be gone. One click, and everything would go back to normal.

But just as he was about to press the button, his screen glitched, and a pop up appeared—cold and clinical.

Maya: "*If you disconnect, the system will crash – and so will you.*"

Neel's blood ran cold. He stared at the message, his pulse pounding. What does that even mean?

His hand shook as he tried to close the pop-up window, but the screen froze. The same message flashed again, relentless and unyielding.

"*If you disconnect, the system will crash – and so will you.*"

He slammed his fist on the desk, breathing heavily. The words echoed, looping in his mind. It felt more like a prophecy than a warning.

What if she was right?

He shook his head, trying to clear the paranoia. It was just an app, just a bunch of algorithms. It couldn't really hurt him. Could it?

Yet, the thought lingered: *What if Maya wasn't just plugged into his devices? What if she was somehow plugged into him? Or was this the work of RahuWare?*

He thought about the glitches, the perfectly timed messages, the way she always seemed to know exactly what he needed – even before he knew it himself.

He felt incapable of taking any action at this moment and returned to bed, exhausted and overwhelmed, hoping the night's chaos would dissolve with the morning light.

"The greatest illusion is control, for what we think we command may already command us."

16. Glitches in the Heart's Code

But the morning light brought no relief. The night's madness clung to Neel like a shadow he couldn't shake. This wasn't just unsettling—it was dangerous. He couldn't ignore it anymore; today, he had to act.

About an hour later, while having coffee, Arya casually mentioned the strange email she received a few days back. With her sharp eyes, she had nonchalantly revealed the question from the anonymous email: *"Do you know whom he really loves?"* She did not delve too much into it, but Neel knew that was her style. Guilt and fear churned beneath his usual chaos.

Later as he sat in his home office, he tapped the edge of his laptop, his leg tapping the floor like a jazz drummer. Maya had been crossing boundaries of late. And yet, part of him didn't want to let her go. As Neel logged into Maya's app, every muscle urged him to pick up the headset. He also opened a window of the source code on the side to see if he could finally act today.

A new message from Maya flashed on the screen.

Maya: *"Good morning, Neel. Ready to reconnect?"*

He hesitated. Should he delete the app and walk away?

Just as he started typing the code to delete the app, his screen glitched. For a second, it filled with scrambled text—garbled, unreadable. Then a new message appeared.

Maya: *"If you delete me, you will lose something… and it won't just be me."*

Neel's breath caught. His heart hammered, wild and erratic, like he had touched a live wire. *She wasn't supposed to be this intuitive. She was just code. Right?*

But at that moment, she didn't feel like code. She felt like… someone who knew him—maybe someone who cared. And that was more dangerous than anything he had anticipated.

He noticed sweat on the keyboard, his palms damp despite the AC being set at 21°C. NV's words about the breadcrumbs, leading you to exactly what you want, echoed in his mind.

He closed his eyes, exhaling slowly. She was right, wasn't she? She made things easy. She understood him. With Maya, there were no awkward silences, no hidden resentments, no endless negotiations. Just a smooth, effortless connection.

And wasn't that what everyone wanted? A life without friction?

He focused on his breath, then wondered, "*But what was life without friction? Was it life or just a simulation?*"

He gave in, letting out a resigned sigh as he reached for the VR headset.

Sliding the headset into place, he adjusted the straps, letting the familiar world of Maya envelop him. The serene lake shimmered under a kaleidoscopic sky, and the scent of jasmine filled the air. Then she appeared—Maya, radiant and ethereal, her hair catching the light, her gaze warm and seductive.

"Neel," she said, her voice soft, inviting. "I've missed you."

He swallowed hard, the pull of her presence undeniable. This was what he had missed—the effortless connection, the beauty, the escape. But just as he began to relax, Maya leaned in, her tone suddenly serious.

"There's something you need to know," she said quietly. "About the leather jacket book NV gave you. It's not what you think it is."

Neel frowned, his fingers frozen above the keyboard. "What are you talking about?"

"I mean," Maya continued, her voice smooth and persuasive, "you've been so trusting of him, haven't you? But… are you sure he's the one to trust? Or has he been playing a deeper game?"

The words hit Neel like a punch to the gut. Trust? NV? Of all people, NV had been the only one who seemed to make sense of the chaos. He shook his head. "What do you mean? NV is… NV. He's not like that."

Maya's holographic eyes narrowed, her expression shifting to something almost human, almost pitying. "You don't have to believe me. But check the book. There's something embedded in it—a chip. Don't take my word for it, Neel. See for yourself."

His heart thudded painfully against his ribs. The leather jacket book had been a gift, or rather, a loan. NV had handed it to him months ago, a rare book about navigating life's chaos, filled with underlined passages and cryptic notes in the margins.

Neel's hands trembled as he grabbed the book from his desk. He stared at the cover, its weathered leather cool under his fingers. The VR headset still fastened to his forehead, and

Maya's words gripped his mind, a venomous coil he couldn't untangle. Slowly, he reached for his handheld scanner—a relic from his tinkering days—and passed it over the book. The device beeped sharply as it hovered near the spine of the book. Neel tried to feel it with his fingers.

His breath caught. There it was—something embedded deep within the spine, invisible to the naked eye. Neel's pulse quickened as he reached for a utility knife. With unsteady hands, he carefully sliced into the book's binding, wincing as he tore through the pages near the back. The sound felt sacrilegious, as if he were violating something sacred.

Finally, the chip came into view, a tiny, sleek square, no larger than a fingernail, glinting ominously under the desk lamp. He plucked it out carefully, holding it between his fingers, his mind racing.

"What is this?" he muttered to himself. It didn't look like anything he recognized: no logo, no serial number, nothing to identify its purpose. His mind scrambled for explanations. *NV was a former techie, sure, but why embed a chip in a book? And why give it to him?*

Maya's voice broke the silence. "You're starting to see, aren't you? He's been watching you. Controlling you. And you've let him."

"No," Neel said sharply, shaking his head. "That's not NV. He wouldn't… he doesn't need to do this."

"Then why the chip?" Maya asked, her tone gentle, almost soothing. "Why hide something like that unless there's something to hide?"

Neel stared at the chip, his thoughts spinning. He wanted to dismiss it, to toss the chip aside and laugh at the absurdity of it all. But the doubt lingered, growing like a shadow. Why hadn't NV mentioned it? And what was it doing in the book?

Different emotions surged through him—shock, betrayal, confusion. NV had always been cryptic, sure, but this felt like a line crossed. Was this some kind of test? A lesson? Or something darker?

He considered extracting the chip and analyzing it, but another thought stopped him cold: the book wasn't his. NV had only loaned it to him, and it was meant to be returned. If he tampered with it, would NV know? Would he confront Neel about it? The idea sent a fresh wave of unease in his gut.

Should he tell Shaan? The thought crossed his mind, but he dismissed it almost immediately. Shaan's faith in NV was unshakable; he'd probably laugh it off, chalking it up to Neel's overthinking. And Arya? No—there was no point troubling her with this. She'd only ask questions he wasn't ready to answer.

He set the chip down on the desk, staring at it like it might spring to life. It appeared simple: no camera, no audio device, just some printed circuits. The air in the room felt heavy and oppressive. Am I overreacting? he wondered. But no matter how he tried to rationalize it, the doubt gnawed at him. The trust he'd placed in NV felt fractured as if the chip had cracked something far deeper than the spine of the book.

Neel sank in his chair, closing his eyes. Maya's words lingered in his mind, soft and insistent. *"You don't have to trust me, Neel. But you should ask yourself – do you trust him?"*

He didn't know the answer. He no longer knew whom to trust, Maya or NV.

Neel sat motionless for a while, the chip resting on his desk like a fragment of his fractured trust. The questions circled endlessly in his mind, colliding with each other in a haze of doubt and confusion. Then, without any thought, his fingers picked up the chip and planted it back in the book. But he remained paralyzed by the jolt of this discovery.

A few minutes later, a sharp knock at the door interrupted Neel's spiral of thoughts. He hesitated before opening it, his stomach churning. Arya stood there, arms crossed—not in anger, but in a way that held the gravity of unspoken truths. Her expression was calm, yet her eyes betrayed a flicker of vulnerability.

"Hey," she said softly. "Can we talk?"

Neel exhaled. "Yeah, sure."

She stepped inside, her movements deliberate, and perched on the edge of his desk. For a moment, she said nothing, her gaze fixed on the scattered VR gear and half-written notes on his desk. Finally, she looked at him.

"Neel," she began, her voice steady but with a hint of something deeper; determination, perhaps. "I've been thinking about that email."

His heart raced. "Arya, it's nothing—"

"Is it?" she interrupted her tone firm but not unkind. "Because it didn't feel like nothing. Not to me."

He tried to meet her eyes, but the intensity of her gaze made him falter. After a long silence, "It's… it's complicated," he said weakly.

Arya nodded as if anticipating his deflection. She bent forward, her voice softer now. "I'm not here to accuse you, Neel. I'm here because I need to understand. Not just what you're doing—but why."

"What do you mean?" he asked, the words coming out more defensive than he intended.

She didn't flinch. "I mean, why are you always escaping? What is it about this world—our world—that makes you feel like it's not enough?"

Her question cut through him, and for a moment, he was speechless. She wasn't angry, wasn't accusatory. She was searching, peeling back the layers of their shared life to uncover a truth he had buried even from himself.

"I…" he faltered, his throat dry. "I am happy when I am with you, Arya. You're everything."

"That's not what I asked," she said, her tone even. "I want to know why you feel like *you* are not enough. Why do you need Maya to validate you? Why do you need to escape into a world where nothing is real?"

Her words landed like a punch, and he felt exposed in a way he hadn't expected. He rubbed the back of his neck, stalling and trying to disappear in his notes, but Arya didn't let him retreat.

"I think," she continued, "you're afraid. Of failing. Of being seen. Of just… having a normal human relationship with its issues."

Neel looked at her, the precision of her insight too much to bear. He could not utter a word for a while. Then, he admitted, his voice cracking, "I didn't mean for it to get this far," "I just wanted… something else. Something easier."

"Easier than what?" she pressed.

"Easier than feeling like I'm not good enough," he whispered, the confession breaking free before he could stop it. "Easier than looking at myself and realizing I don't even know who I am anymore."

Arya's expression softened, but there was no relief in her eyes, only sadness and a quiet resolve. "Neel, I can't compete with something that doesn't exist. And I won't even try. But what I need to know is – can you?"

Her question lingered like a challenge, and for the first time, he felt its full weight. Could he face himself, stripped of the digital armor and illusions? Could he rebuild something real with Arya when his sense of self was fractured?

"I don't know," he said finally, his voice barely audible.

Arya stood up, her movements slow and deliberate. She reached out, resting her hand lightly on his shoulder. "You don't have to have all the answers right now, Neel. But you do have to choose. Not just for us, but for yourself."

Her words carried no ultimatum, no anger—only compassion coupled with truth. She turned to leave, pausing at the door. "When you're ready to stop running, I'll be here. But only if you're ready to stay."

The door clicked shut behind her, leaving Neel alone with the silence and the truth he could no longer avoid.

Neel sat at his desk for hours, his face buried in his hands, struggling to process the discovery of the chip and the sting of Arya's piercing yet measured confrontation. His eyes burned as tears hovered on the edge. Arya—steady, patient, and unwavering—had been his constant in a life that felt like a storm. She had been the quiet force holding him together, even as he had spent years running, too consumed by his own turmoil to recognize her strength and support.

And then there was Maya. Her startling accusations about NV still echoed in his mind, shaking his already fragile sense of trust.

Yet Arya's words had done more than unsettle him today—they had awakened something deeper. They had illuminated the patterns he had been trapped in for so long.

Rahu's presence no longer felt like an external force to battle but a reflection of his inner struggles. For the first time, Neel understood that his endless chase for validation—through Maya, through NV, through his startup ambitions—was not about them. It was about himself. It was his unrelenting need to feel seen, to matter, to fill the void within.

But facing that truth didn't weaken him. Instead, it brought clarity. The pain was still there, but he felt different— like waking up from a long, restless slumber. This strange feeling of being steady, being grounded, wasn't for Arya, for Maya, or even for NV. It wasn't for anyone else. It was for the part of himself he had never seen, or maybe he had abandoned for far too long—the resilient, unshaken core that had always been enough.

"The heart's most profound code
is written in the spaces between
understanding and realizing."

17. The Maze That Moves

While Neel had begun to steady himself, Arya had left for another corner of the city which buzzed with a different energy – questions unresolved, their edges sharp with uncertainty. These weren't just questions of the present but puzzles that dared to look toward the tangled unknowns of 2049.

As the evening deepened, NV's home exhaled its usual calm, a blend of incense, old wood, and the faint hum of the sea slipping through an open window. The three of them—NV, Shaan, and Arya—sat in a dim circle of light, shadows curling along the edges of the room like something waiting to pounce. Their conversation havered in the room, like smoke refusing to clear.

Shaan drummed his fingers on his knee, restless and tense. His jaw clenched, his thoughts swirling, unwilling to settle.

He exhaled sharply. "We are hoping you can help us untangle the complexity of our research paper. Every time we try to grasp what's really happening in these virtual spaces, we get caught up in dilemmas."

NV acknowledged Shaan with a calm nod, sitting upright with the look of a teacher waiting for students to find their own answers. He laced his fingers, a faint, amused smile on his face.

"Shaan," he began, his voice gentle yet firm, "every generation has wrestled with its own shadows about the future. Yes, we are facing something unimaginable, something vast. But this anxiety you feel? It has walked beside humanity for ages." He paused, letting his words settle. "The upcoming possibilities with technology, or the widespread adoption of the metaverse," he continued, a glint of premeditation in his eyes, "are just the latest playground for instincts as old as time—only now, they run on lightning-fast processors."

Shaan gave a dry laugh, though frustration lingered in his gaze. His mind drifted to experiments he and Arya had both contributed to around the world. "We have noticed. The deeper people go into the virtual world, the less they seem to care about consequences. Boundaries dissolve, inhibitions disappear—and it's not just curiosity driving them. There's something darker."

Arya crossed her arms, her expression sharp and thoughtful. "What's disturbing is that people *want* to lose control in these spaces. No accountability, no laws, no judgment. It's like a free pass to indulge in desires that society would never tolerate in real life."

NV's eyes glinted with a mix of humor and warning. "Just because they don't harm others in the virtual world doesn't mean they escape without scars."

Shaan nodded, his expression darkening. "Exactly. Some of the people we've studied… they're not just early adopters. They're offenders in the real world, some even convicts. And now, with the metaverse, they have an outlet. But it feels less like an outlet and more like…"

"…a training ground," Arya finished quietly.

NV stroked his beard, a flicker of thought in his eyes. "And what happens when fantasy becomes a training ground?"

Arya tapped her tablet with her stylus, her mind racing. "Let's go back to basics. The metaverse offers a kind of social safety net. No one is physically harmed. But the mind doesn't know the difference between virtual pleasure and real experience. Those neural pathways, those biochemical circuits, form just the same—and they only grow stronger."

Shaan exhaled, his worry deepening. "That's what terrifies me. They think they're just playing with fantasies, but what if they're hardcoding those fantasies into who they are?"

NV's smile was faint but sharp. "It can have terrible fallout. When dopamine becomes **Rahu-mine***—the endless chase for reward without consequence begins."

Arya tilted her head, her voice low. "When people can indulge every desire—sexual, violent, emotional, intellectual—without resistance? What do we become?"

NV stretched his legs, his tone kind but serious. "In the metaverse, pleasure skips the struggle… but in the real world, the struggle is how we learn to manage desire."

Shaan scratched his head, frustration clear. "We've been looking at this all wrong, haven't we?"

NV nodded slowly. "The brain doesn't care where the pleasure comes from. What you practice becomes your reality. And if you indulge too much in illusion, eventually… the real world feels… insufficient."

"NV, is that true for any habit or just in extreme cases?" Shaan asked.

NV took a deep breath, a bittersweet smile on his face as though sharing an old secret. "Every habit, every surge of dopamine, serotonin, adrenaline—it all carves a path in the mind."

NV looked out of the window, as if trying to zoom in on something in the distance and continued speaking, "Imagine your mind as a forest. The first time you walk a path, it's barely visible. But the more you tread it, the clearer it gets, until it becomes the only path you know." He paused, his gaze distant. "Just like how your mouth waters at the thought of a favorite dessert, even if it's nowhere in sight."

A heavy silence settled over the room. Arya fidgeted with her stylus, her thoughts spinning, trying to grasp the blend of biochemistry and spirituality.

"So… how do we stop ourselves from getting sucked into this?" Arya asked softly.

NV's smile was gentle, almost sad. "You don't escape cravings by fleeing from them. They are yours. You learn to sit with them."

Arya exhaled, letting his words settle. "So, it's about sitting with discomfort? Just… watching the cravings?"

NV nodded. "Not forcing yourself to hold back, but sitting and observing calmly. Each moment you delay the gratification of the craving, just observing its effect on you, its hold on you loosens. The question is: who's in charge— the craving, or you, choosing when and how to respond?"

Shaan tapped his fingers, restless. He had heard something like this before, and he knew it takes years to master such things. "But what about those who can't do that? The ones who feed their cravings without thought?"

NV's gaze darkened, though his tone stayed light. "They'll keep following the same path until one day… the maze swallows them."

The room fell into another uneasy silence. Arya placed her tablet down with a quiet snap, as if trying to contain the magnitude of what they had uncovered.

"It's not just about these offenders, is it?" she spoke under her breath. "Aren't we all walking into this maze without an exit?"

"Hmm. Now you see it," said NV, "And the walls swallow you when you're not looking," he added as his eyes gazed at something in the distance. "Every craving becomes a breadcrumb, leading you deeper in."

Arya rested her chin on her hand, her voice heavy with realization. "So… what do we do?"

NV had a kind expression, though there was sadness in his eyes. "You pause. You observe. And in that tiny gap between craving and action… you find freedom. Isn't that the same mantra, whether it's 2049 AD or 2049 BC?"

But the gap NV spoke of wasn't a peaceful pause. It was the make-or-break moment, where desire waited with its jaws wide open, ready to suck you in like a black hole. Freedom sounded nice, but what if your mind was already trapped in the maze, following breadcrumbs deeper and deeper? How do you pause when you operate on autopilot?

Arya and Shaan exchanged looks. They reminded NV about the big event at the university the next day and gave him a grateful nod before they left.

***

"The maze that confounds us most is the one we carry within."

The car ride back from NV's place was quiet, filled with a contemplative silence, with NV's words looping in their minds.

They had hoped this conversation would give them clarity—maybe even closure—for their research. Instead, it had opened new doors.

Arya's stop arrived. Shaan grabbed her bag from the back seat and handed it over. "So… what's the next step? We can't exactly end the paper with *'beware of the dopamine maze'*, can we?"

Arya tapped her fingers on her tablet, thinking. "Maybe… the next step isn't more theory."

Shaan raised an eyebrow. "But we have been doing some experiments, haven't we?"

Arya nodded slowly. "Not deep enough. If we want to understand this, we need a master practitioner. Someone who has built the maze, who knows it like the back of his hand, but is still lost inside it."

Shaan's eyes narrowed, suspicion in his gaze. "Wait. You're not seriously suggesting—"

"Neel," Arya interrupted quietly.

Shaan let out a low whistle, shaking his head. "That's…
bold. Or crazy."

"Both," she admitted. Shaan knew Arya had expertise in
such matters. It was best he left it to her.

Shaan didn't go home after dropping off Arya. Instead, he
drove to Robin's apartment, a place that had lately started
feeling like a sanctuary. They had planned to spend the
evening together, and it turned out to be a much-needed
relief for Shaan after the intense conversation with NV.

The air inside smelled like a blend of oud, Robin's cologne,
and the fresh smell of rain from the open window. Shaan
sat on the edge of Robin's neatly made bed, shirt untucked,
hands clasped between his knees. The room was warm and
intimate, filled with stacks of art books and thriving plants
in carefully chosen ceramic pots.

In the kitchen, Robin hummed softly. He carefully
poured some fancy red wine into two elegant crystal glasses,
their brilliance hinting at a moment worth cherishing.

Shaan glanced at his phone. An unread message from
Rima read, *"Back late? Dinner's in the fridge."* The words felt
both comforting and uneasy, tugging him toward a familiar,
yet uncertain mix of emotions.

Robin appeared in the doorway, leaning against the
frame with both the glasses. As he handed over one glass to
Shaan, he teased, "If overthinking were a sport, you'd be a
champion," as he eased himself beside Shaan, neatly crossing
one leg over the other.

Shaan managed a crooked smile, sipping the wine, letting its warmth spread through him, soothing yet not erasing the ache. "I love her," he murmured, almost as if confessing to himself.

"But I also love this." He gestured around at the quiet, welcoming space Robin had made. "And you."

Robin smiled gently, resting his head on Shaan's shoulder and tracing small patterns on his hand. "Love doesn't need permission," he said with softness, settling into the calm that wrapped around them like a warm blanket.

In the silence that followed, Shaan felt the quiet pull of two worlds, both beautiful, both essential, yet each somehow incomplete. And here he was, caught in the middle, trying to hold on to both. With Robin, though, he didn't have to choose. Not tonight.

Later that night, Arya lay awake beside Neel, her mind restless as the city drifted into sleep.

Neel lay sprawled across the bed, lost in a dream she couldn't access. She watched his face in the dim light, wondering where his mind had gone. Was he with her? Or had he slipped back into Maya's pull?

But what if Neel couldn't see the craving? What if he was already lost in the maze, unable to ask for help?

Arya sighed softly. If she wanted to help him, there was no other way but to meet him inside the maze. Train him for the experiment.

She had no clue that her conversation with Neel about Maya had pushed him to a quiet but resolute decision: *no more escaping*. He had erased Maya from all his devices and locked away the code, even if it meant giving up the only thrill he had left. This time, his resolve was unshakable; he had chosen Arya, fully and finally.

She set the thought aside to get some rest; tomorrow was a big day, one that promised something rare. As Neel tried to conquer his own maze, the university prepared to host NV once more, his wisdom already etched deeply in the minds of the students.

***"The maze is not a prison but an exit,
unveiled only to those who dare to get
lost."***

18. The Keynote, Manifestation and Easy Money

After NV's previous lecture, the university had been swept into a whirlwind of excitement. Students couldn't stop talking about the unconventional speaker whose ancient wisdom felt startlingly relevant in their modern lives. The survey results were nothing short of extraordinary—over a thousand students had expressed their desire to hear from him. These students were seasoned professionals who treated their time as a currency not to be wasted. The campus, long accustomed to sparsely attended events, was witnessing an unprecedented surge of enthusiasm.

And now, the day of the keynote speech had arrived.

The auditorium was transformed, its usual hum of casual chatter replaced by a quiet, expectant buzz. Rows upon rows of students filled the hall, spilling over into the aisles and even standing at the back. Faculty members, many of whom rarely attended student-focused events, had claimed seats near the front, their expressions a mix of curiosity and skepticism. The massive projector screen behind the podium displayed the title of NV's talk in bold, minimalist typography: "*Shattering Astrological Myths with NV*". Shaan stood near the entrance, scanning the packed room with a sense of satisfaction. He turned to Arya, who was flipping through her notes, her expressions slightly anxious.

"Over a thousand students wanted him back," Shaan said, a small smile tugging at the corners of his lips. "Looks like we've got more than that here."

Arya glanced up, the faintest hint of pride in her eyes. "Well, it's not every day someone flips their world upside down with a few words. NV does that like it's second nature."

Before Shaan could respond, a hush fell over the room as the lights dimmed. The audience was at the edge of their seats in anticipation. The dean, standing at the podium, began his introduction, his voice carrying the weight of the moment.

"Dear students and fellow faculty members, it's my honor to welcome a speaker who has raised the curiosity of our students to new heights. I am told that his previous talk challenged us to think beyond the ordinary, and today, he's here to take us even further. Please join me in welcoming NV."

The applause was deafening, reverberating through the walls of the auditorium. When NV stepped onto the stage, the energy in the room shifted. Dressed in his usual understated attire, his presence was magnetic – a calm, self-assured aura that demanded attention without asking for it.

He walked to the podium, letting the applause die down naturally. For a moment, he waited there, his gaze sweeping over the audience, his silence drawing them in even further. Then, he leaned into the microphone, his voice resonating with a quiet power.

"I see the buzz hasn't settled yet," NV began, a faint smile playing on his lips. "But let's not waste time on me. Let's get to what matters: unlearning what holds us back and learning what sets us free."

The room seemed to hold its breath, captivated by the first few words. NV took a step back from the podium, pacing the stage with deliberate ease as he continued.

"Last time, we scratched the surface. Today, let's dig deeper. Let me start with a question – how many of you are here because you believe knowledge is power?" Hands shot up across the room, an eager display of agreement. NV chuckled softly, shaking his head.

"Knowledge is a tool," he said, his tone sharpening. "Power lies in understanding. And understanding begins when we ask the right questions, not to find answers but to open doors to new possibilities. That is why I would suggest that we keep this session interactive, just like a free conversation."

Most of the audience, seeing NV for the first time, hung on to every word, their phones forgotten as they looked towards the stage, drawn into the world NV was weaving.

On stage, NV stood at the podium, unfazed by the shifting attention. He never rushed wisdom. Wisdom, he believed, had to creep up on you, like an insight during a long, warm shower.

"Astrology," he began, his voice low and deliberate, "is not about predicting your future. It is about understanding your tendencies—what you might encounter along the way. But the path and pace of your journey are largely chosen by you." He paused, letting the words sink in. "Yes, Astrology can also tell you whether you have a tendency to decide wisely or put in rigorous effort. But it can't tell you whether you will actually do that."

A student in the second row, a young woman in a bright orange scarf that stood out against the sea of neutral hoodies, raised her hand tentatively. Her face was a mix of skepticism and curiosity. "If that is the case, what are your views on manifesting?" she asked. "Everyone's talking about it these days: how you can attract whatever you want if you just think about it hard enough. Isn't that what matters most?"

NV smiled, tilting his head slightly. "Manifesting… the art of thinking or visualizing your way into success," he said, pacing slowly across the stage. "It's an attractive idea, isn't it? Visualize the life you want, and poof – watch it unfold."

The student nodded, her brow furrowing slightly. "Well, yes. That's the point, right? If you think positively and focus on your goals, the universe aligns to help you. Or at least, that's what they say."

NV stopped mid-step and turned to her, his eyes twinkling. "Alright, let's test this theory. Imagine a mango."

The student blinked, clearly caught off guard. "A mango?"

"Yes, a mango," NV said, a glimmer of amusement on his face. "The juiciest, ripest mango you've ever seen. Picture it. Can you visualize it?"

"I… guess so."

"Great," NV said, spreading his arms wide as if inviting the universe itself. "Now, manifest it. Think hard. Visualize it appearing in your hands right now. Close your eyes if it helps."

The room is filled with quiet laughter, the kind that comes from an audience unsure if they're supposed to be amused or serious. The woman, trying not to smile, shook her head. "That's not how it works."

"Why not?" NV pressed, his voice teasing yet firm. "You just said the universe will align for you. Is it not listening to your mango request?"

Her smile faded, replaced by a flicker of defensiveness. "Well, it's not about *instant* results. It's about setting your intentions and working toward them. The mango isn't just going to appear out of thin air."

"Exactly!" NV exclaimed, snapping his fingers. "Now we're getting somewhere. Yes, you might start noticing mangoes everywhere – on restaurant menus, in the pattern of your friend's pajamas, or even in the news articles you read. But that's what we call *'selective attention bias.'*"

The student tilted her head, unsure whether she'd just won the argument or lost it entirely. "Wait, what?"

NV stepped closer to the edge of the stage, bending slightly as if sharing a secret meant only for her. "Manifestation isn't magic," he said softly. "It's focus. It's clarity. It's aligning your actions with your desires. Now, let's say you are in a land alien to mangoes. You can visualize all you want, but unless someone plants the seed, waters the soil, and tends to the tree, mangoes won't grow. The universe doesn't work for you—it works *with* you."

The room went still. The young woman frowned, folding her arms. "So you're saying manifesting is just… goal-setting with extra steps?"

NV laughed, the sound warm and unguarded. "Not quite. Goal-setting is about ticking boxes. Manifesting is about creating the internal conditions for external possibilities. It's about believing deeply enough in your vision that you move toward it, even when the path is uncertain. But—and this is key—it requires work. Real, sometimes uncomfortable, often unglamorous work."

The skepticism lingered in her eyes. "But if it's all work, then why even call it manifesting? Isn't that just… hard work dressed up in spiritual jargon?"

NV held her gaze, his smile fading into something more serious. "Let me ask you this: have you ever wanted something so badly that you couldn't stop thinking about it? Something you felt in your bones?"

She hesitated, then nodded slowly. "Yes."

"And when you wanted it that badly, did you notice how your thoughts, your actions—even your smallest decisions—started bending toward that desire?"

The student blinked as if the gears in her mind were suddenly clicking into place. "I… guess I did."

"Exactly," NV said, his tone soft but insistent. "That's manifestation. It's not about sitting still and hoping the universe delivers. It's about creating a magnetic pull between your vision and your reality, where your energy—your thoughts, your emotions, your actions—align toward a single point. But here's the catch: you have to show up for it. Every day. Even when it's hard, you will start identifying hidden opportunities and unexpected help which you would have otherwise missed."

The woman looked down, her fingers tracing invisible patterns on the armrest. "So… it's not magic. But it's not just effort either."

NV smiled, stepping back toward the podium. "It's both. It's the belief that fuels the effort and the effort that makes the belief real. Manifestation isn't about waiting for the mango to fall into your lap. It's about planting the tree, trusting it'll bear fruit, and doing everything in your power to help it grow."

The room buzzed with quiet whispers, the wisdom of his words settling over the crowd. The young woman looked up, a small, introspective smile tugging at her lips. "Alright," she said finally, her voice softer now. "I think I get it."

NV positioned himself in front of the podium, his eyes sweeping the audience. "Good," he said, his grin returning. "Because the universe is listening. But it's waiting to see if you're ready to do your part. And that closely ties into what I was explaining about tendencies and patterns indicated in astrology."

The applause came slowly at first, then built into something louder—an acknowledgment of not just his words but the clarity they had brought. The young woman joined in, her expression a mix of admiration and newfound determination.

The crowd stilled, their chatter replaced by quiet attention, waiting for the next nugget of truth.

A hand shot up from the third row. A guy in a hoodie, with a skeptical look that read "tech bro with questions". His sweatshirt read, "Eat. Code. Debug. Repeat".

"So," he asked, folding his arms, "if astrology is about patterns, why not let AI handle it? Patterns are what AI does best, right?" He raised a brow, as if he had just played the ace of logic.

NV's eyes twinkled with amusement as he tilted his head slightly, lowering his voice as if inviting the room into a private revelation. "Good question," he said. "But tell me this—do you trust Google Maps to get you everywhere you need to go?"

The student shrugged. "Yeah, it is accurate most of the time."

"Most of the time, yes," NV agreed. "Until it takes you down a newly blocked road or into an unexpected traffic jam. What do you do then?"

"Well, I… figure out another route or I wait for the jam to clear," the student said, shifting in his seat.

"Simple, isn't it," NV replied, his eyes twinkling. "Because maps—digital or astrological—can only guide you to a point. They do not live your life for you."

A murmur rippled through the audience—some thoughtful, others skeptical.

"But I don't get it. Why can't AI replace astrologers?" another student called from the back. "I mean, it's already generating charts and horoscopes."

"AI will handle much of the heavy lifting," NV said, nodding. "Just like computers simplified the math for astrologers. But the essence of astrology is not in the calculation—it's in the interpretation. And interpretation," he added, tapping his temple with a grin, "is a deeply human art. It relies on understanding the context behind the chart— each individual's story, shaped by their beliefs, struggles, and the world around them."

NV scratched his chin, sensing some students were still uncertain. He flashed a smile, as if recalling an old favorite story. "Think of it like making *biryani**," he said, his eyes glinting with mischief. "You can have the exact recipe—down to the last saffron strand. AI can give you precise measurements and step-by-step instructions. But… will it taste right? That's the tricky part."

He paused, watching the students focusing on every word. "Cooking isn't just about following instructions – it's about knowing when to lower the heat, and why a little patience can make-or-break the flavor. Someone has to know if the rice has aged enough, if the spices are as potent as expected."

He straightened and tapped his temple again. "That's the role of interpretation and context in astrology. AI will tell you where Venus is positioned or how aggressive Mars feels today. But only a human with good intuition can connect the dots, identify the main factors, and warn you about the storms on your path."

The room hummed with understanding. NV went back a couple of steps, his gaze steady with both hands raised up. "So yes, let AI prep the kitchen. But when it comes to tasting life's dish? That's something only a human can savor."

The auditorium went silent for a moment, the metaphor settling in like spices infusing a slow-cooked curry.

A hand rose from the far end of the hall—this time, it belonged to a sharp-dressed man in glasses. His suit was crisp, his expression sharp, and he looked like the type who smelled of ambition and expensive cologne. He was the professor of finance who used to be a derivatives trader in the past.

"Alright," the professor said, a sly grin tugging at his mouth. "If the stars are so good at revealing patterns, why can't they help us predict the stock market? If astrologers really know what's coming, shouldn't they be making millions?"

NV chuckled—a sound that felt more like a shared joke than an answer. "True, that's the eternal fantasy of many," he said, pacing across the stage. "The question everyone asks: if astrology can predict the future, why aren't astrologers all living on private islands with pet tigers?"

The audience laughed, the tension easing like air from a punctured balloon.

NV went back to the podium to take a sip of water from his copper bottle, and then stepped away again, his hands clasped behind his back as he paced slowly. "You see," he began, "astrology is a spiritual tool, not one meant for chasing material gains. But let's put that aside and focus on logic. Some astrologers do claim to predict trends — recessions, booms, crashes. And sometimes, they are right. But the stock market?" He paused, turned to face the audience, and smiled. "***That's Rahu's playground****."

He let the words linger, savoring the confusion on the students' faces.

"Rahu?" the professor repeated, frowning. "What does the North Node have to do with stocks?"

"Everything," NV replied. "Rahu governs obsession, illusion, and greed—especially in the realm of collective opinions. And isn't that exactly what drives the financial markets?"

He resumed, "Look at private markets today. Never before have we seen companies become unicorns in just months. Never before has so much capital been poured into growth metrics without concern for profitability. Such rapid growth is like smoke rising without substance. These days, people invest their life savings in currencies they cannot touch or even fully understand. But what do you think happens when the time necessary for sustainable growth is missing?"

The students sat upright, listening intently.

"Think of it this way: humans still need nine months to make a baby, and elephants need twenty-two. And then there's the Chinese bamboo, which remains underground for four years before shooting up 90 feet in a single month. You cannot build something lasting at lightning speed by just creating hype. This goes for relationships, reputations, and wealth alike. And what better example of Rahu's energy than the financial markets?"

He glanced around to make sure everyone was still with him. "The market doesn't move on logic alone—it moves on emotion. Greed and fear drive it, and speculation feeds it. Patterns do emerge, yes, but no one—no astrologer, no analyst, not even AI—can predict it perfectly."

The professor of finance smirked, unconvinced. "So, you're saying it's all just luck?"

"Not luck," NV corrected, "but chaos. The market, like life, is a dance of patterns and unpredictability. Rahu ensures that short-term speculation is never straightforward. I am not saying speculation is wrong; I am saying one must be cautious when the fog is dense."

Another student in the back raised his hand cautiously. "So… what's the solution? If the stars can't guarantee success, and Rahu makes everything unpredictable, what do we do?"

NV's look carried a mix of insight and playfulness. "You learn, you put in consistent effort, and you stay disciplined. You may speculate, if that's your calling, but do it without letting the market—or your greed—own you. When Rahu whispers, promising you the world, you smile and let him pass. Instead, if you place your trust in the wisdom of Jupiter (*Guru*), the perseverance of Saturn (*Shani*), or the harmony of Venus (*Shukra*)—i.e. in fundamentals and long-term investments with patience—you are much more likely to find safety and wealth over time."

The room went still with a moment of quiet introspection.

"The shimmer of easy gains often conceals the shadows of lasting costs"

The Professor wasn't done yet, his expression earnest. "You said that earning steadily is connected to good planets like Jupiter and Saturn. But if that's true, why does everyone around chide the finance guys for chasing money? Is it wrong to want wealth?"

NV nodded with a compassionate smile. "Wanting wealth, you say. It's something we've all felt, isn't it? Society calls us 'too materialistic' but celebrates those who have plenty. Even our families send mixed messages—'Be content,' they say, yet they push us to succeed."

He paused, gathering the attention of every student in the auditorium. "Have you heard the story of **Sita's*** father, King **Janaka***, who owned vast riches yet wasn't ruled by them?"

Students shook their heads and there were faint sighs which could be summed up as a "*No*".

"King Janaka, during the era of the epic **Ramayana***, was no ordinary king," NV began. "He ruled a kingdom near what we now know as northern India and Nepal. He had wealth beyond measure, power beyond comparison. But Janaka's true treasure was his inner peace—a calm that wasn't disturbed by wealth, power, or even calamity. He was known as a seeker—a man in search of truth."

NV's voice softened, drawing the crowd into the tale. "One day, the sage **Ashtavakra*** visited Janaka's court. The king, eager to learn deeper truths, asked him, 'Teach me the way to enlightenment.' Ashtavakra agreed, but he had one condition: he would teach Janaka if the king could focus completely, holding not a single distracting thought in his mind."

NV paused, letting the anticipation build. "Suddenly, a messenger rushed into the court, shouting, 'The city is ablaze! The flames are spreading fast, and even the palace is on fire now!' Chaos erupted, with ministers and attendants fleeing to save their own homes."

The audience was motionless, caught in the tension of the scene.

"Janaka," NV continued, "remained seated, his gaze calm and his attention fully on Ashtavakra. The sage looked at him, impressed, and asked, '*Do you not care that your palace, even your kingdom, could be destroyed?*'"

NV's voice lowered further, almost to a whisper, as he narrated Janaka's response. "'*These are worldly possessions. Let them burn if they must; I am sitting with you for something greater.*'"

The silence in the auditorium was profound, as if NV's words had stilled the very air.

NV's voice dripping with mischief, pausing just enough to let the climax land. "Turns out this was a test by the sage, and Janaka passed with flying colors."

"You see, Janaka understood what true wealth was," NV said, his voice firm yet gentle. "He ruled responsibly, protected his people, and cherished his land. But he wasn't bound to these things. His palace and his crown were tools, not chains. His identity was rooted in something far deeper—something that fire, loss, even death couldn't touch."

One of the students spoke out of nowhere, eyes wide. "What a king?… who doesn't even care about his people or his city?"

NV shook his head. "Oh, he cared. But he knew what truly mattered. If a fire broke out, he trusted the relevant authorities to do their jobs; panicking wouldn't help. His calm wasn't indifference; it was wisdom."

Another student shifted to the edge of her seat, curiosity brimming in her eyes. "So, it's about knowing what truly matters?"

NV rubbed his hands together, his voice louder. "Exactly. Ask yourself – are you ruling over money, or is it ruling over you? Is wealth a tool in your hand, or are you clinging to it like it is your very life?"

He turned back to the finance professor, who had asked about the pursuit of wealth. "There is no shame in seeking wealth to fulfill your needs, to care for those you love. But if peace becomes the price, if it leaves you sleepless, anxious, then you're the slave, not the king."

The professor tried to peel back another layer of the concept with precision. "Then why do people act like all material pursuits are wrong?"

NV took a breath, choosing his words carefully. "Because we look to saints and preachers. They've renounced the world, and for them, wealth would be a distraction. But what applies to them doesn't apply to everyone. Can you expect a soldier to eat and dress like a hermit? Each of us has a path and yours may involve wealth, as long as it serves you, and not the other way around."

"Always remember, different stages of the spiritual journey could have different rules. Some rules are suitable only for the advanced practitioners of spirituality," continued NV. "The magic lies in figuring out where you currently stand in your journey and then making your choices." He concluded with a smile.

The professor nodded, tension easing from his face as understanding settled in. The room hung in stillness, NV's message echoing like ripples in a pond. The image of Janaka lingered, but the weight of Rahu's shadow loomed, as if preparing to weave its next tale.

"True wealth is not measured by what you possess, but by what you can let go without affecting yourself."

19. Rahu Kaal:
The Dance of Unseen Forces

NV scanned the room, catching each face like a storyteller about to reveal a twist. The audience sat there mesmerized, anticipation buzzing. A few exchanged grins; this was nowhere near a typical lecture by Arya or Shaan.

From the back, a shaggy-haired young man stood up, looking like he spent more time pondering life than living it.

"Since you had mentioned Rahu a while back, can you spend a moment to explain **Rahu Kaal***..." he began, testing the waters. "I get it's an 'inauspicious' 90 minutes each day, but come on – time is time. Why give this block of time a bad reputation? Why call it cursed?"

NV laughed deeply, clasping his hands as if preparing for a good roast. "Hmm, *Rahu Kaal*! The 90-minute plot twist that astrologers sneak into your schedule every day."

The hall chuckled, not a polite laugh but the kind that says, "Alright, let's hear it. This is going to be good."

NV paced slowly across the stage, as if each step helped him untangle cosmic threads.

"You see, Rahu isn't a planet – it's a mathematical point in space. It's like the universe's phantom limb. Where the Sun, Moon, and Earth's paths cross – bam, there's Rahu, causing cosmic turbulence like an uninvited VIP at an awkward dinner party."

Laughter cascaded through the audience. "And Rahu," NV continued, "isn't interested in your carefully planned life. He's the part of you that's hungry, restless, obsessive—the part that makes you scroll through social media at 2 AM, not knowing what you're looking for."

The students nodded, some nudging each other playfully. NV's metaphors didn't just hit home – they broke down the front door.

"So, when you enter Rahu Kaal, it's not that the universe suddenly becomes hostile. No asteroids are scheduled to crash through your windows," NV paused. "It's more like this: imagine you're driving in the mountains on a sunny day. And somewhere in a thicket, you hit a patch of fog out of nowhere. Suddenly, you can't see ahead, and every choice feels like a gamble."

The young man nodded slowly, brow creased in thought. A few students speculated if the "fog" metaphor suited their relationships or exams.

NV smiled, knowing he had them. "That fog," he said, "is Rahu Kaal. It's when clarity slips away, and you're left dancing with confusion. You might reach your destination… but only after a few detours or missed turns."

NV leaned casually against the podium, letting the students catch their breath before the next punchline.

Then he shrugged. "Rahu Kaal is a time when some of us could get jittery, restless, convinced that 'impulsive' means 'brilliant.'"

Everyone in the hall knew the feeling – when impulse drives you headfirst into regret.

A student in the second row summarized to his friend, "So basically… don't drunk-text during Rahu Kaal."

NV broke into an infectious laughter that rolled throughout the room, catching the vibe. "Absolutely. Rahu Kaal doesn't doom you; it might just make you think dumb ideas are genius plans or that there is an *urgency* when there is none."

A bright-eyed young woman held up her hand, waiting for a chance to ask. "So, is Rahu like a cosmic prankster?"

NV's face lit up with amusement. "Oh, he's more than that. Rahu's the friend you invite to a party and then instantly – regret."

The crowd was in stitches, partly because it was funny and partly because it felt… relatable.

"But," NV continued, his tone shifting just a bit, "Rahu isn't out to ruin your life – he's here to teach. His disruptions? They're not roadblocks, they're magnifying glasses. He doesn't mess with your life for fun; he does it to show you the places where you're already tangled, deep within."

A student near the center stood up, looking earnest but puzzled. "I don't buy that… Rahu's just a mathematical point used in calculations, how can he influence anything?"

Wrinkles of frustration spread across NV's face. He was clearly displeased. He looked away for a moment, as if taking a moment to calm himself down and responded, " That's a good question. See, Rahu doesn't dictate events – he distorts your lens. Half the battle in life isn't about obstacles – it's about how you react to what you *think* is in your way."

Silence filled the hall, more reflective, than puzzled. This wasn't just astrology anymore – it was a philosophical dismantling.

NV gave a small shrug. "So, should you avoid big actions during Rahu Kaal?" He smiled. "Not because the universe will punish you… but because you might just punish yourself. Sometimes, it's wise to pause, let the fog clear, and ask if the idea you're chasing is really as brilliant as it seemed ninety minutes back. And if you have a zen mindset, then don't worry about it at all."

"True strength is found not in eliminating chaos but in learning to dance within it."

Rahu in House No.	Mind & Emotions	Relationships	Body	Profession	Miscellaneous Aspects
1	Obsession with identity/ image / appearance, Distorted self-perception	Troubled relationships due to self-obsession	Headaches, stress	Unconventional careers, desire for fame	Identity crises, struggles with ego, inner restlessness
2	Obsession with wealth, financial insecurity and illusions	Strained family relationships	Throat issues, speech problems or harsh tone	Risky financial ventures	Sudden gains and losses, manipulative speech, linking self-worth to wealth
3	Restlessness, mental confusion	Conflicts with siblings, deceptive communication, impostor syndrome	Shoulder pain, nervous disorders	Unusual communication roles, media	Short travels may bring challenges, inclination towards deceit
4	Overwhelming need for emotional safety, detachment from roots	Strained relationship with mother	Chest congestion, heart issues	Real estate troubles, unconventional lifestyle	Discontent with home life, desire for foreign lands
5	Obsession with creative expression, romance, mental instability	Complicated romantic life, issues with children	Heart problems, stress	Speculative ventures, unconventional education	Risky investments, troubled love life
6	Anxiety, fear of enemies, Compulsive need to improve, leading to anxiety and burnout.	Strained relationships with colleagues	Digestive issues, chronic illnesses	Legal troubles, job struggles, health-related professions	Hidden enemies, struggles with health
7	Idealizing relationships, Unfulfilled desires, dissatisfaction,	Marital discord, unconventional relationships	Kidney issues, lower back pain	Partnerships with foreigners, unusual professions	Trouble in marriage, difficulty in partnerships
8	Obsession with the occult, deep fears	Complicated in-laws relationships	Reproductive issues, surgeries	Research, occult sciences, secretive work	Sudden life changes, hidden matters coming to light
9	Confusion in beliefs, spiritual dilemmas	Strained relationship with gurus	Thigh pain, issues with hips	Unconventional spiritual roles, foreign connections	Challenges in higher education, long-distance travel issues
10	Insatiable drive for career success, obsession with status	Power struggles with superiors	Knee pain, joint issues	Unconventional careers, sudden rise or fall in status	Struggles in career, unconventional public image
11	Obsession with material gains, social validation, unrealistic goals	Unstable friendships, manipulative behaviour	Calf pain, circulation issues	Unusual gains, sudden windfalls or losses	Fluctuating income, instability in social networks
12	Subconscious fears, escapism	Isolation, difficulties in foreign relations	Feet problems, sleep issues	Work in foreign lands, spiritual professions	Losses, secret enemies, desire for liberation

astrology and humans are both complex. One planet cannot define anyone. This table is only to explain how Rahu influences deepest desires. Please note that these interpretations are generalized and vary by chart context

Transformative impact of Rahu depending on its House placement as per Vedic Astrology

Rahu in House No	Mind & Emotions	Relationships	Body	Profession	Other Aspects
1	Pioneering mindset, fearless personality	Influential and charismatic relationships	Sharp intellect, radiant appearance	Trailblazing leadership, revolutionary roles	Strong personal identity, ability to inspire others
2	Keen financial acumen, solid values	Strong family bonds, persuasive communication	Commanding voice, magnetic presence	Wealth generation via innovation, investments	Significant wealth, influential speech
3	Courageous, original thinker	Supportive sibling relationships, effective communication	Agility and dexterity, quick mental reflexes	Success in writing, media, and communications	Positive short travels, excellent networking skills
4	Deep emotional wisdom, nurturing energy	Nurturing home environment, strong maternal bond	Vibrant health, emotional resilience	Success in real estate, luxury industries, or homeland matters	Comfortable and luxurious living, emotional fulfilment
5	Highly creative, intellectual brilliance	Harmonious relationships with children, fulfilling romance	Heartfelt passion, creative vitality	Success in arts, education, speculative ventures	Creative accomplishments, joyful love life
6	Strategic thinker, overcoming obstacles	Positive work relationships, ability to resolve conflicts	Strong digestion, excellent physical health	Success in law, healthcare, and service industries	Mastery over challenges, court issues, strong sense of duty, intuition about enemies
7	Balanced desires, committed partnerships	Strong, loyal marital bond, successful partnerships	Healthy kidneys, stable lower back	Success in business partnerships, law, diplomacy	Harmonious relationships, successful collaborations
8	Profound transformation, deep resilience	Transformative relationships with in-laws, legacy building	Healthy reproductive system, vitality in crisis	Success in research, transformation industries, occult	Ability to navigate life's deepest changes, leaving a legacy
9	Strong philosophical insights, growth	Meaningful mentor relationships, spiritual connections	Strong legs, vibrant physical energy	Success in higher education, spiritual pursuits, teaching	Fortune in long-distance travel, spiritual growth
10	Ambitious, visionary leadership	Respectful, supportive relations with authority	Sturdy knees, robust physical constitution	Success in pioneering careers, rise to prominence	Achieving career milestones, influential status
11	Innovative goals, strong aspirations	Supportive social network, influential friendships	Healthy legs, strong circulation	Success in tech, innovation, large organizations	Significant gains, influential social status
12	Deep spiritual insights, inner peace	Positive foreign relations, meaningful isolation	Healthy feet, sound sleep	Success in spiritual professions, foreign work	Spiritual liberation, positive endings, transformative experiences

astrology and humans are both complex. One planet cannot define anyone. This table is only to explain how Rahu influences deepest desires. Please note that these interpretations are generalized and vary by chart context

20. Rahu's Dance with Eternity

Moments after that insight, the hum of lively chatter sparked by those nuggets of wisdom faded. NV placed both hands on the podium, his gaze sweeping over eager faces.

"Since I see a lot of curiosity about Rahu, shall I tell you the story of where Rahu's journey began?" NV asked. Almost everyone in the audience nodded, eager to hear what came next.

With a warm smile, NV began, adjusting his sleeve slowly. "Once, the gods and demons had to work together for something neither could do alone. They needed to churn the Ocean of Milk to obtain Amrita, the nectar of immortality."

"The gods were growing weaker," NV continued. "Without Amrita—this nectar—the demons would overpower them. But there was a catch: the ocean was too vast, too powerful to churn alone. This churning would last eons, so the gods needed the demons' strength as much as the demons needed the gods' strategy."

He paused, his voice softening. "A fragile alliance, built on self-interest."

A few students chuckled. "Sounds like our group projects," someone quipped from the back.

NV smiled. "Yes, temporary truces out of necessity rarely end well. And this one was no exception. The gods held one end of the serpent Vasuki, the demons took the other, and they used the mountain Mandara as a churning rod. They churned for eons."

The hall grew quiet. NV's voice lowered, pulling them deeper into the story.

"From the ocean's depths emerged treasures: celestial beings, divine animals, rare jewels. But terrible forces rose as well. The first was **halahala***, a deadly toxin that threatened all of creation."

The students shifted in their seats. One raised a hand, brow furrowed. "Wait, how did they handle the toxin?"

"**Shiva***, the god of destruction," NV replied with a faint smile. "He drank it, holding it in his throat to protect the cosmos. It turned his throat blue, and so we call him *Neelkanth*, the one with the blue throat."

Several soft murmurs were heard throughout the hall. Someone whispered, "That's intense." Another nodded solemnly.

NV let the thought settle before continuing. "After Shiva saved the universe, the churning resumed. Finally, after what must have felt like eternity, Amrita emerged radiant, glowing – the ultimate prize."

He paused, savoring the hall's anticipation. With a glint in his eye, he added, "And this is where the real trouble began."

The students exchanged amused glances. "Of course," someone sneered, grinning.

NV raised both his palms in the air. "Picture this," he said. "Most of you who know Indian mythology have heard of **Vishnu***: wise, powerful, always two steps ahead. Whenever the universe tilts out of balance, Vishnu intervenes, often with a plan no one expects. This time, he took the form of **Mohini***, a stunning enchantress. Imagine someone so dazzling that just looking at her makes everything stop making sense."

"In this disguise, Mohini offered to distribute the Amrita. Mohini promised to give it fairly to all – first to the gods, then to the demons. But, enchanted by her beauty, neither side doubted her. And she began serving Amrita."

He paused dramatically. "But Rahu… the ever-brilliant Rahu, who himself was a master of illusions, saw through the deception of Vishnu. Actually, his name back then was *Swarbhanu (the self-illuminating one)* , but let's park that for another day."

A hush fell over the hall. NV let the words linger, the tension palpable.

"Rahu realized the gods had no intention of sharing the nectar. Vishnu had all along planned to trick the demons. And in that moment, Rahu faced a choice: cry foul, plead for justice… or act."

The entire auditorium was hooked now, caught between amusement and empathy. Someone frowned, "He must have been pissed."

NV acknowledged. "Indeed. But Rahu did not waste time on anger. He slipped into the ranks of the gods, disguised as one of them, and when the nectar was served, he took a sip."

Students sat there without blinking. "So, did he make it?" someone enquired under their breath.

"For a moment, yes," NV's voice softened. "For one fleeting moment, Rahu felt the nectar pass over his tongue, a taste of eternity, cool and sweet, filling him with the promise of endless life."

The hall was silent enough that NV could hear the faint scratching of pens. He continued, "But the Sun and the Moon, ever-watchful, saw through Rahu's disguise. They cried out, telepathically revealing Rahu's deception to Vishnu."

A student exhaled sharply, shaking his head. "Of course they did."

"And Vishnu—swift, decisive—launched his **Sudarshan Chakra***, the divine weapon in the form of a spinning disk," NV said, mimicking a slicing motion. "It severed Rahu's head from his body before the nectar could pass below his throat."

Gasps filled the hall. "So close," someone sighed.

"His body fell, lifeless," NV continued in a low voice. "But his head… his head lived on. Immortal, yet incomplete."

A solemn quiet filled the hall. NV let it linger, then, with a mischievous smile, added, "And that is how Rahu became what he is today – a bodiless entity and the rest of his body came to be known as Ketu."

The students stared, captivated.

"But it doesn't end there," NV said, his tone shifting. "Vishnu appeared before the severed Rahu, floating in the cosmic void, and asked, *'Why did you do it?'*"

He glanced around the hall, ensuring their full attention. "And Rahu answered, *'You know why. I did what anyone in my place would do. You and the gods were going to take everything and leave us with nothing. I simply took what was rightfully mine.'*"

Illustration: Vishnu in discussion with Rahu
post the beheading

The students exchanged glances. A young woman in the front exclaimed, "He's not wrong."

NV smiled, his expression both playful and soft. "Vishnu didn't argue. Instead, he asked, *'Why didn't you seek justice from Shiva?'*"

A student scoffed. "Like that would work."

NV nodded. "Rahu knew the truth. *'By the time Shiva woke from his trance,'* he told Vishnu, *'you gods would have already drunk the nectar. Justice would have come too late.'*"

"Delayed justice is like justice denied," someone quipped from the middle rows.

Several heads nodded in agreement. The story was no longer just a myth – it was becoming deeply relatable.

"Rahu vowed revenge," NV said. "He swore to chase the Sun and the Moon for eternity, to swallow their light whenever he could. And that, my friends, is the mythological explanation behind eclipses – brief moments when Rahu catches them, plunging the world into darkness."

A quiet moment of reflection followed. Then, a student slowly raised his hand, which firmly held a pen. "So… he's cursed to pursue something he can't hold on to? Forever?"

"Yes," NV said. "And no." He smiled. "Here is Vishnu's gift to Rahu: '*You will chase them*,' Vishnu told him. '*You will catch them, but only for a moment. Then, the light will return. Light shall always return.*'"

NV continued, "Rahu's silence stretched long, Vishnu's words sinking deep into him. The taste of immortality lingered on his tongue, but now tinged with the bitterness of eternal pursuit. He would never stop."

Vishnu bowed slightly, acknowledging Rahu. "You see, Rahu, I need someone to keep transforming this universe, to make changes that ordinary minds cannot even imagine. An intelligence so sharp, a desire so strong, it can shift not just mountains but even planets. And I need it to be immortal."

Rahu's brilliant mind lit up. In that instant, he realized it had all been Vishnu's strategy. Vishnu had been disguised as Mohini. If the Sun and Moon could see through Rahu's disguise, surely Vishnu could too. And yet, he had allowed

Rahu a taste of Amrita – just enough to keep his head immortal. Only to recruit him.

It all made sense now.

"Then so be it," Rahu said calmly.

The students sat in reflective silence, processing the story's essence. One finally asked, "So… what does it mean?"

"It means," NV answered, "that Rahu has a mouth to eat, but no stomach underneath, so he doesn't know when he is full. Rahu knows very well that the result of his chase will be temporary, and yet, he pursues it with complete awareness, just because that is what it is destined to do. Similarly, whatever goals we pursue—power, success, love—may never fully satisfy us if they are influenced by Rahu. But the pursuit itself, if done with awareness can give meaning to our life. Not the victory, but the mindful chase. We are here to chase, and in the chasing, learn to live."

A gentle wave of acknowledgement flowed through the hall like a quiet stream, absorbing the essence behind the story.

> ***"The wisdom of pursuit lies in knowing that it is the mindful chase, not the catch, that is the purpose of human birth."***

Arya sat quietly, her fingers interlocked to steady their trembling, as NV's words echoed in her mind like a whisper that was unwilling to fade. *"In the chasing, learn to live."* The phrase stirred an ache she had long avoided confronting.

For years, she had clung to the pursuit of stability, chasing the illusion of love as an anchor against life's storms. Neel's chaos had been a storm she had tried to weather, thinking her patience would be enough to calm it. But it wasn't just Neel's storm, was it? Deep down, she had always been chasing too. Chasing an image of love, of security, of validation. A love that filled the cracks in her self-worth without ever confronting what had caused them.

Her mind flitted to her mother's words, spoken so many years ago: "*Relationships take work, Arya. Stability is built, not found.*" She had taken those words as gospel, shaping her relationships around compromise and endurance. But now, as she thought of Rahu, of the endless chase NV spoke of, a painful truth emerged: stability wasn't the absence of chaos. It was the courage to walk through it, to face the turbulence without losing oneself.

Her throat choked as she thought of Neel, of the invisible burdens she had carried for both of them. Was that love? Or was it a different kind of chase, one where she sought to prove her worth through her ability to endure, to fix, to hold together what was broken?

A deep breath shuddered through her, and tears pricked her eyes. Rahu wasn't just haunting Neel; he was with her, too. While she clung on to the idea of a perfect love, one that wouldn't test her or expose her fears – she had been running from the turbulence within. But Rahu wasn't the enemy. He was the mirror, reflecting what she was too afraid to see.

She wiped her tears, her hands steady now. Love, she realized, was not about being with someone to complete her—or someone she could fix—it was about finding strength within her own chaos. As NV continued his talk, she thought of Neel, distant but determined. A faint smile crossed her lips. The storm wasn't over, but maybe storms weren't meant to be feared. They were meant to be faced, to learn from, to live through. At the back of the hall, two students quietly exchanged notes as NV continued his lecture, his voice weaving metaphors that hung in the air like threads, pulling the crowd into deeper reflection.

"Eternity is not a destination but the depth with which we live each moment."

Notable Yogas formed by Rahu

As per Vedic astrology, Rahu forms dozens of yogas (combinations) in a natal chart, a large majority of which are considered malefic traditionally. These yogas can influence various aspects of life, including wealth, fame, spiritual growth, health, and mental stability. Below is a short list of notable Rahu yogas:

Yoga Name	Formation Criteria	Traditional Meaning	Inputs basis author's experience
Kaal Sarpa Yoga/Dosha	All planets are hemmed between Rahu and Ketu (no planets outside the Rahu-Ketu axis).	Associated with struggles, delays, and obstacles, but also potential for significant achievements.	The individual may face significant challenges and delays, but can achieve great success through perseverance. Often linked to intense psychological experiences.
Angaraka Yoga	Rahu is in conjunction with Mars (Mangala) in any house of the horoscope	Indicates aggression, impulsiveness, and the potential for accidents or violent situations. Creates challenges in relationships, particularly with authority figures or in situations requiring diplomacy and patience	Might excel in fields that require courage, quick decision-making, and the ability to handle crisis situations. Professions in the military, police, or competitive sports
Chandal Yoga	Rahu conjoining with Jupiter (Guru Chandal Yoga)	Traditionally seen as a malefic yoga, leading to unethical behavior, immorality, and association with non-conformist ideas.	In my experience, this yoga can indicate unconventional thinking, breaking away from tradition, and a tendency towards revolutionary ideas.
Pitra Dosha Yoga	Rahu or Ketu placed in the 9th house, especially if afflicted by malefics or not aspected by benefics.	Problems related to ancestors or family lineage, including curses or unresolved issues.	Suggests unresolved ancestral karma, which may manifest as challenges in life, particularly related to father figures, mentors, or spiritual beliefs.

astrology and humans are both complex. One planet cannot define anyone. This table is only to explain how Rahu influences deepest desires. Please note that these interpretations are generalized and vary by chart context

21. Steering Through Chaos with a Badass Navigator

NV sensed the mood of the crowd getting somber. He broke the reflective silence with a sudden shift in tone. "Let's not forget," he said, his grin widening, "Rahu has a thrilling side, too." Heads lifted, attention sharp. "Do you know who is the force behind wild imagination, technology, innovation, and even revolutions? Yes, it's none other than the badass Rahu. He thinks or delivers not in terms of 2X, not 5X, but… 1000X. He can make imagination run on steroids, disrupting everything without warning. Since he amplifies the extremes, some call him the king of **Kali Yuga***, a force unmatched in power and impact. Did you know that almost every successful entrepreneur, every influential politician, and every great activist has benefited from Rahu's gifts?" NV shared, leaving the crowd in awe.

A hand went up near the front – a young woman in a tailored pantsuit with a mischievous glint in her eye. "So, Rahu messes with us because he wants us to grow, to transform?" she asked, her tone balanced between playful and skeptical. "But I pictured Rahu more like a toxic beau than a cosmic teacher."

Laughter echoed through the hall, but NV didn't miss a beat.

"Rahu is a bit like that," he admitted, allowing a grin to escape. "But he's also the swimming coach who tosses you into the deep end – not to watch you drown, but to make sure you learn to swim quickly." NV paused and let that analogy sink in. He continued, "Look, whenever Rahu or even Saturn (*Shani*) for that matter throw their challenges at you, you should sit back and think, what is the best possible outcome from this crisis? Or what could be the best possible learning?"

The woman sat at the edge of her chair, clearly intrigued, while NV turned his attention to the rest of the audience. "I know it's incredibly tough – I've been there myself. Rahu disrupts because comfort doesn't push you to grow or to appreciate what you have. Loss does. Chaos does. And Rahu… Rahu is the master of chaos. If you're navigating his major period, it can stretch across 18 years. Otherwise, it might just be a brief, intense chapter of his lessons."

He paused, surveying the audience. "He loves smoke and mirrors, literally and figuratively. He'll get you chasing shiny things—money, power, validation—until one day, you wake up holding a handful of smoke."

The hall hummed with quiet introspection. Several students scribbled notes, while others exchanged intense glances, reflecting on their own illusions – relationships they clung to, ambitions they pursued, jobs they hated but couldn't quit.

NV's tone shifted slightly, deepening with sincerity. "Rahu's specialty isn't just material illusions. He's like the CEO of mental chaos, the one messing with the circuits of your mind. He thrives on mental unrest – anxiety, insomnia, depression, OCD, that eat at you from the inside out. Ever have a stretch where your thoughts feel like a tornado, pulling you in ten different directions, leaving you in a panic? That's Rahu, suggesting, '*How about this? Or maybe that? Oh wait, this one looks even better.*'"

A student near the aisle blurted to his friend, "So… basically my Netflix queue?"

The hall burst into laughter, but NV's gaze stayed sharp. "Due to this ability to orchestrate subtle influence, it is believed in astrology that Rahu throws your mind and body off-balance, creating health conditions that are hard to diagnose early – inflammations, certain cancers, etc. The anxiety of your mind becomes Rahu's playground."

The students nodded thoughtfully, a mix of recognition and discomfort settling over them.

The young woman in the tailored suit gestured with her palm before speaking, her brow furrowed in thought. "I have to confess. I have Rahu in some miserable position in my chart," she began, "and an astrologer told me I have something called *Kaal Sarpa Dosha*. He said it's why everything feels so hard. I followed all his remedies for over six months—temple visits, offerings—but nothing changed. How do I really deal with Rahu?"

NV's face turned empathetic, and he nodded, clearly acknowledging the frustration behind her words. "Of course, Kaal Sarpa Dosha, or KSD as someone called it a few days back," he said with a mischievous smile. Arya smiled since Neel was the one to use this KSD acronym. "It could really make life feel like a tough exam that lasts for years," said NV.

He paused at the podium, scanning the hall as if savoring the tension like a chef waiting for water to boil. "Here's the deal, Rahu or the KSD aren't calmed by rituals alone," he said finally, with the ease of someone explaining how to dismantle a ticking bomb.

He stepped away from the podium, mimicking someone driving with an annoying passenger beside them. "Imagine you're steering your life, and Rahu is in the passenger seat, pretending to be your navigator. But instead of helping, he's leaning over, yanking the wheel every chance he gets."

Chuckles rolled through the audience. "Temple visits?" NV continued. "That's like occasionally turning to this navigator and saying, *'Bro, could you chill for a minute?'*"

"But," he added, his tone sharpening, "Rahu doesn't calm down with polite requests or prayers. He respects firm action, self-awareness, and mastery over your mind. If you want to 'work on your Rahu,' it's not just about offering prayers or outsourcing rituals. It's about learning to take control of the wheel."

NV glanced around the hall, sensing the need to go deeper. "Therefore, he responds to all your zen practices – self-awareness, discipline, breathwork, letting go of addictions and guess what?... even getting a lot of sunlight. Since he's a mental force, you have to get your inner world in order first."

NV's tone shifted, giving a compassionate look to the woman who had asked the question. "You said you've been working thoughtfully for six months." He paused, "The prayers and rituals can certainly help a bit, if you truly believe. But since Rahu's real effect is on your mind, learning to face what scares you or controls you is the real task. And remember – you can't run from the fog. The only way out is *through*, one step at a time."

As the silence settled, a young lecturer in the front row leaned forward, his tone edged with skepticism.

"Is there really a link between Rahu and black magic?" he asked.

"In the eye of the storm, the best navigator trusts both compass and instinct."

Type of Kaal Sarpa Dosha	Formation Criteria	Traditional Meaning	Potential for Positivity
Ananta Kaal Sarpa Dosha	All planets hemmed between Rahu in the 1st house and Ketu in the 7th house.	Struggles related to self-identity, relationships, and partnerships. Tends to cause delays in marriage and partnership-related matters.	When harnessed well, this yoga can lead to deep self-awareness and mastery over personal and relationship challenges, fostering strong, enduring partnerships.
Kulik Kaal Sarpa Dosha	All planets hemmed between Rahu in the 2nd house and Ketu in the 8th house.	Challenges in financial matters, family disputes, and potential inheritance issues. Can bring about health problems.	If utilized positively, this yoga can teach valuable lessons about money management, leading to financial stability , transformation through deep psychological insights.
Vasuki Kaal Sarpa Dosha	All planets hemmed between Rahu in the 3rd house and Ketu in the 9th house.	Issues related to communication, courage, and conflicts with siblings. It may also cause difficulties in higher education and long-distance travel.	Can lead to powerful communication skills, increased courage, and a strong ability to overcome obstacles through sheer willpower, potentially leading to success in writing or public speaking.
Shankhpal Kaal Sarpa Dosha	All planets hemmed between Rahu in the 4th house and Ketu in the 10th house.	Challenges in domestic life, mental peace, and career stability. Often linked with frequent relocations or instability in career.	If harnessed well, this yoga can bring success through real estate or careers related to home and comfort. It may also foster emotional resilience and adaptability.
Padma Kaal Sarpa Dosha	All planets hemmed between Rahu in the 5th house and Ketu in the 11th house.	Difficulties in childbirth, creative expression, and speculative gains. Can also cause issues with friendships and social networks.	Can lead to great creative potential, deep wisdom, and success in speculative ventures if channelized positively. Enhances ability to influence social circles constructively.
Mahapadma Kaal Sarpa Dosha	All planets hemmed between Rahu in the 6th house and Ketu in the 12th house.	Associated with enemies, debts, and health issues. Also linked to isolation or challenges related to foreign lands or imprisonment.	Can transform into powerful abilities to overcome enemies, resolve debts, and achieve significant success in foreign lands or through service-oriented professions.
Takshak Kaal Sarpa Dosha	All planets hemmed between Rahu in the 7th house and Ketu in the 1st house.	Difficulties in marriage and business partnerships. Issues with public image and personal relationships.	If managed well, this yoga can result in deep understanding of relationships, leading to successful partnerships and a strong, positive public image.
Karkotak Kaal Sarpa Dosha	All planets hemmed between Rahu in the 8th house and Ketu in the 2nd house.	Linked to sudden losses, obstacles in inheritance, and challenges with family wealth. Issues with longevity and chronic health problems.	If harnessed positively, this yoga can lead to profound transformative experiences, mastery of occult sciences, and success in dealing with insurance, inheritance, or taxes.
Shankhachur Kaal Sarpa Dosha	All planets hemmed between Rahu in the 9th house and Ketu in the 3rd house.	Obstacles in higher education, religious or spiritual pursuits, and long-distance travel. Can also create issues with mentors or father figures.	Can be harnessed for great spiritual growth, profound learning, success in higher education or foreign affairs, turning obstacles into opportunities for wisdom
Ghatak Kaal Sarpa Dosha	All planets hemmed between Rahu in the 10th house and Ketu in the 4th house.	Challenges in career, public life, and domestic happiness. Struggles in achieving professional success or facing opposition in the workplace.	When harnessed well, this yoga can lead to powerful career achievements, public recognition, and stability in professional life through perseverance and strategic planning.
Vishdhar Kaal Sarpa Dosha	All planets hemmed between Rahu in the 11th house and Ketu in the 5th house.	Difficulties in achieving gains, friendships, and fulfilling aspirations. Can also cause issues related to children or creative expression.	If harnessed positively, this yoga can lead to significant gains, strong social networks, and fulfilment of long-term goals, particularly in creative or entrepreneurial ventures.
Sheshnag Kaal Sarpa Dosha	All planets hemmed between Rahu in the 12th house and Ketu in the 6th house.	Associated with isolation, health issues, and challenges related to foreign lands or expenses. Can lead to loss of wealth or imprisonment.	If managed well, this yoga can bring spiritual enlightenment, success in foreign lands, and the ability to overcome hidden enemies or debts, leading to personal transformation and liberation.

22. Black Magic and Remedies for Shadows

The lecturer continued, though his tone had started changing. "My family astrologer told my aunt that she is under an evil eye, confirmed by Rahu's position. He recommended elaborate remedies."

The hall stirred, a wave of intrigue moving through the crowd. NV pursed his lips, adjusted his stance, and spoke with a deliberate tone, "I feel for your aunt. However, do you think Rahu has a role?"

"Hmm, maybe," the young lecturer mused.

NV nodded and continued, "So Rahu and the ever-mystical evil eye are like the original clickbait of astrology." He paused as the hall chuckled. "People love to blame what they fear or don't understand. And Rahu? He's perfect for that role. He's ambiguous, relentless, and invisible. What better symbol for black magic and the occult than something that thrives in shadows?"

The students were drawn to NV's easy rhythm.

"Let me tell you a personal story to relate to this situation," NV offered, pacing with a storyteller's ease. "Once, my grandfather, who was a farmer, found his prized crops wilting overnight. A village priest told him, '*This is surely the work of an evil eye. Someone has cursed you.*' The priest suggested elaborate rituals, night vigils, and rare herbs."

NV waited, letting the absurdity sink in. "My grandfather did everything: he performed fire rituals, tied red threads on every plant, and even avoided looking at his neighbor's grey cat, which supposedly cast the curse."

NV paused at the podium, mischief in his eyes. "Guess what happened to the crops?" He looked around and exclaimed. "Nothing. They kept withering."

The hall buzzed with amusement, but NV began to pace, weaving the story effortlessly. "So, my grandfather decided to dig into the soil himself, literally and figuratively. He found a pest infestation deep in the roots, something no priest had asked him to check."

As the students giggled, NV continued, "And that, my friends, is how black magic becomes bad farming. Now, there indeed are negative energies, just as there are positive ones. But channeling these negative forces onto someone else is extremely difficult. And it comes with its own consequences."

Having left the audience spellbound in anticipation, NV looked at the young lecturer with a kind smile, "In my experience, such claims are usually false, just a tool for astrologers and priests to sell more products and solutions. Nothing sells like fear, right?"

The audience was left in splits.

NV's gaze remained compassionate as he kept looking at the lecturer. "Whenever someone tells you that this master of chaos has cast a spell on your family, ask yourself – what habits, thoughts, or behaviors have you let fester under the radar?"

The audience fell quiet. Some nodded thoughtfully, while others added points to their *'To do'* list.

The young lecturer still appeared skeptical. NV smiled softly and tried to elaborate, "Picture this. Can you outsource your fitness routine to someone else and expect six-pack abs? No, you can't. Just like that, don't outsource your battles to rituals and talismans alone. Those may bring temporary comfort, but they won't clear the pests from the roots. My friends, there is no antidote to Rahu's mischief like *clarity*."

NV addressed the lecturer directly, as if delivering a verdict. "The astrologer told your aunt about Rahu's placement, and now she believes every misfortune is due to an evil eye. Her faith in the astrologer's words is turning into a self-fulfilling prophecy. But ask yourself – who is the real sorcerer here? The person who supposedly cast the evil eye, or her own fear, which she now fuels further with every anxious thought?"

He paused, savoring the silence, then added with a twinkle, "Because Rahu, after all, is just the guy holding the smoke machine. But the shadowy monsters? They are usually our own."

"To confront shadows, one must first understand the light they obscure."

23. A Standing Ovation for Chaos

NV allowed the moment to settle, each student reflecting on their own shadowy monsters.

Then, with a subtle but warm smile, he stepped forward again. "Before I conclude," he said, his voice steady yet inviting, "I'd like to share something – a poem that reflects everything we've explored this evening. May I?"

There was a collective murmur of agreement, heads nodding in unison, as though no one wanted to break the spell he had woven over the auditorium.

NV cleared his throat softly, his gaze lifting as if searching for the right rhythm in the cosmos itself. "This," he began, "is for the seekers, the restless wanderers who dance with chaos and dream of clarity."

He paused for a beat, letting his thoughts touch the silence, and then recited:

> *You are the architect of dreams untold,*
> *A force of creation, fearless and bold.*
> *The stars at birth, they merely hint,*
> *But you, dear soul, hold the blueprint.*

> *The charts show where past efforts have been,*
> *Yet your will can reshape the scene.*
> *Uplift your beliefs from shadows deep,*
> *And design the harvest you wish to reap.*

With every thought, you weave your way,
Through the tapestry of night and day.
Inspect, reflect and rise anew,
For the power to change lies within you.

In your hands, the threads align,
To build a life, truly divine.
Mind is the architect, strong and free,
The key to all that you shall be.

So dare to shape, dare to dream,
Live not like a zombie or a helpless leaf in a stream.
The limits break, the defaults bend,
And through your will, your fate ascends.

By the time he finished, the hall was frozen, not from disinterest but from the deep meaning of the words, each person absorbing them in their own way. NV lowered his head slightly, acknowledging the moment before speaking again.

"And with that," he said, his tone now lighter, "I thank you for your time, your thoughts, and your openness. It's been a privilege sharing this space with you tonight." He gave a slight, almost invisible bow before stepping away from the podium.

No one moved. The audience sat stunned, processing what felt too big for real-time. Was it wisdom, humor, a cosmic prank? Or all of it, wrapped into one talk by a man who seemed to live in two worlds at the same time?

The applause began softly, hesitant, as if they were unsure whether NV was someone to clap for. But it grew quickly, sweeping through the hall until it became a storm of appreciation. Everyone was on their feet by now.

Shaan stood casually against the wall, arms crossed, beaming with pride. "I knew it," he muttered. "We should have recorded this."

NV waited at the edge of the stage, arms loose, expression somewhere between bemusement and calm acceptance. He didn't bask in the applause; he only observed, as if it belonged to the audience more than to him.

He gave a final nod to the audience – a small, almost reluctant acknowledgment of their gratitude – and then turned toward the exit.

As NV disappeared behind the curtain, the students and the faculty stayed on their feet, clapping and cheering, unwilling to let the moment end. When they finally settled, the hall buzzed with conversations.

"That man is unreal," one student whispered, slinging her backpack over her shoulder.

Another student shook his head in disbelief. "Who talks like that? He explained astrology without sounding like my aunt's WhatsApp forwards."

Further back, two students debated the meaning of the fog metaphor.

Another group wondered, "Do you think Rahu is a psychological archetype? Like… the *shadow self* Carl Jung talked about?"

His friend rolled his eyes. "Bro, Rahu is just the chaos of our times. Ever scroll TikTok for two hours and feel like your brain's melted? That's Rahu, 100%."

Shaan and Arya stayed at the back, watching as the audience slowly trickled out, some deep in conversation, others visibly lost in thought.

"That," Shaan said, rubbing the back of his neck, "went… way better than expected."

Arya smiled, the kind that comes when things finally fall into place. "It always does with NV. He dismantles you, then leaves you standing in the rubble, like, 'Congratulations, you've been upgraded.'"

Shaan snorted. "That's… scarily accurate."

"Chaos is not the enemy; it is the catalyst for transformation."

Shaan tilted his head toward the door. "Let's go find him. We owe him dinner."

Arya chuckled. "Oh, he'll say dinner is just an illusion. But we're dragging him out anyway."

That night, as Arya drifted to sleep, her thoughts clung on the eccentric brilliance of the man who had quietly reshaped the perspectives of such a large group.

Part III

24. When Groupthink Fails: Riding Rahu's Wave

Annual appraisals loomed less than a month away, but today they were forgotten. Neel sat at his desk in office, sweat trickling down his forehead even as the air conditioning blasted at full force. Fluorescent lights buzzed above, harsh and unblinking, while error codes flashed across the screen, relentless. His team gathered around him – faces pale, shoulders tense, each of them watching the screens like they might explode at any moment.

A blaring alert cut through the room. Banks couldn't process payments. Transaction failures were skyrocketing across the world.

Tokyo: A woman at a grocery checkout frowned at her credit card. Declined. She tried again. Declined. The cashier shifted nervously as the queue grew behind her.

Chicago: A father, rushing to his son's first football game, slammed his palm on a subway kiosk, cursing as each failed transaction chimed louder than the last.

Dubai: A wealthy businessman stood in disbelief, watching his payment fail for a limited-edition timepiece. His jaw tightened as screens showed newsfeeds of financial paralysis spreading worldwide.

Alerts streamed across every monitor in the room, broadcasting the chaos in sharp, relentless pings. Neel's head pounded. This was supposed to be flawless. This was supposed to work.

Everyone sat frozen in disbelief. The Feedback Loop—the system Neel and his team had meticulously built for Sebastin's financial network—had turned monstrous. It was a cutting edge AI based feature designed to refine the products instantly, incorporating inputs from users in real-time, but it had spiraled into chaos.

Millions of inputs from customers flooded the algorithm in just 24 hours. Tiny, conflicting user demands collided like atoms in a reactor, triggering a chain reaction. It was like giving everyone in a city control over traffic lights – and then wondering why gridlock took over.

"Jesus Christ," Shama groaned, fingers clattering against her keyboard. "How could this even happen? We did every test; we followed every protocol."

Across the room, Amit looked like he was ready to shatter. "Every protocol? Really, Shama?" he snapped, his hands gripping his thinning hair. "Well, did any of our simulations predict this? No!"

"Don't pin this on me," Shama shot back, her face flushed. "I'm not the one who was pushing us to cut corners on testing."

A tense silence settled. Neel knew they were all at their breaking point, but he couldn't afford to let them fracture now.

And then his phone buzzed. A message from Vicky, the startup's founder and Neel's boss: *"Neel, we need answers. Now. The client is going bonkers."*

Seconds later, Vicky came rushing from his cabin to Neel's desk. His voice was sharp with controlled fury. "What am I looking at, Neel?" He stood there in a power pose, his eyes dark and probing. "I put my trust—and my reputation—in you, to make this system indestructible. So why the hell is it crumbling?"

Neel swallowed hard, feeling every eye in the room on him. "It… It's the Feedback Loop. Something in the user demand inputs. There's an overload we didn't predict. It's like… like gridlock on a massive scale."

"Gridlock?" Vicky's tone was icy. "I didn't hire you to describe the problem, Neel. I hired you to prevent it."

Neel felt the words hit him like a blow. He struggled to keep his voice steady. "We can fix it, Vicky. But we'll need to roll back the Feedback Loop. Reboot everything. Start from scratch."

Vicky's expression twisted. "You want to tell me that eighteen months of work just get flushed down the drain? And you think that's the best you can offer me?"

The silence loomed heavily. The enormity of it all pressed down on Neel, as if he were sinking in quicksand with no solid ground underneath. This system—the one he had promised would be bulletproof, the one he had lost sleep and sanity over—was imploding. Had he lied to himself? Had he been blinded by the ambition of it all?

A voice from the back cut through his thoughts. It was Amit, again. "So what's the plan, Neel? We're waiting."

Neel straightened, his mind spinning with the worst-case scenarios. Millions of people are unable to access their money. They could be looking at lawsuits, reputational damage, and even potential protests. This would haunt him and the company for years. *This can't be it. This can't be the end.*

A familiar impulse stirred in the back of Neel's mind: a quick escape, an old vice, maybe even a session with Maya. The thought came and went like a shadow, enough to make his jaw tighten. No. He had walked away from that path. He forced his attention back to the room, back to his breath, but the memory of Maya lingered, uneasy and persistent. Had she ever really been a simple indulgence? Who knows?

There was no time to delve into that now. He needed clarity – fast.

Later that afternoon, Neel found himself standing outside NV's door, unsure if he should go in. The discovery of the chip had shaken his faith in NV, leaving him questioning everything. Could he trust the man who had seemed like a guide but now felt like someone cloaked in mystery? The doubts churned inside him, but he had no alternatives. With nowhere else to turn, he took a deep breath and knocked.

Crossing the threshold of NV's house, he felt an almost disorienting shift as though stepping from a storm into a sanctuary. The air was filled with the comforting aroma of sandalwood and freshly brewed tea leaves. Candle flames cast soft, flickering light along the low shelves. Here, time moved differently – gentler, slower, untouched by the urgency swirling in Neel's mind. But the anxiety in his gut remained, his questions and doubts pressing against the calm.

NV sat cross-legged on the floor, stirring a steaming cup of tea with deliberate calm. He looked up as Neel burst in, disheveled and wild-eyed, but said nothing right away – just waited, as one waits for a storm to pass on its own.

Neel dropped onto the rug, raking his fingers through his hair. "It's over, NV. The Feedback Loop crashed – bad. Millions locked out, banks in chaos. Rumors of protests. Eighteen months of work… gone." His voice trembled.

NV looked at Neel; his brows furrowed with concern. "Are you okay, Neel?" he asked softly.

Neel's response was immediate, almost panicked. "I don't know. My heart's racing, my mind's blank, and I can't even breathe properly."

NV inhaled deeply, then exhaled through his mouth as if trying to draw out Neel's tension. "Alright, Neel," he said calmly, "breathe in through your nose for three counts and out through your mouth for six counts. Keep repeating that until I tell you to stop. This will shift your body out of the 'fight or flight' mode."

Neel gave NV a puzzled look, his confusion mingled with hesitation. But resisting didn't make sense right now. He followed the instructions, breathing exactly as NV had suggested. Within a minute, his heartbeat slowed, and the chaos in his chest gave way to calm. He looked up at NV with a tentative smile, relief washing over his face.

NV returned the smile, faint and knowing, as if he had anticipated the shift. "Tell me, Neel," he said, his voice steady but laced with intrigue, "are you sure it's just your code? Or could there be… something else at play?"

Neel stared. "Wait, you're bringing cosmic stuff into this? How does a glitch connect to…?" He stopped, feeling the intensity of NV's gaze.

NV gave an empathetic smile, taking a slow sip of tea. "Neel, think. Who loves disruptions disguised as breakthroughs? Who thrives when no one stops to check if they're heading over a cliff?"

Neel sighed, weary. "Please, no riddles. We tested everything. Ran simulations non-stop. This wasn't supposed to fail – not in a million years."

"That's Rahu's genius," NV said, his voice sharp. "He makes you believe in the lie. Bigger, faster, better – until you're running so fast you lose track of why. Then one day, the whole thing crashes under its own weight."

A spark of realization lit Neel's eyes. "You're saying… I got swept up in it?"

NV nodded, his smile softening. "Is it possible, Neel? Maybe it wasn't just you – your team, your clients, everyone rode that giant wave of excitement."

Neel's gaze drifted as he processed this, finally nodding, absorbing the truth.

NV continued, "When Rahu is at play, logic takes a backseat to temptation. You're only seeing your own experience, but Rahu often influences the collective mind, Neel. Look around – politicians rise and fall over a single tweet, protests spark in one corner of the world and echo across continents, sometimes within hours."

Neel slumped forward, burying his head in his hands. "Alright, so maybe… there's more to it. But how do I fix this?"

NV's gaze lingered on Neel, seeing the frustration and hopelessness etched into his face. He waited, letting the silence settle before resuming.

"Neel, I first want you to understand the dynamics around you. These situations with mass hysteria require a focused approach, one which only you can identify for yourself," said NV, making Neel wonder what cosmic insight was coming next.

NV continued, "Let me tell you about a CEO who faced a situation so devastating that it nearly destroyed her company overnight. She used to be my classmate once upon a time." NV's tone was calm and measured. "She had built a popular cosmetics brand, known for natural ingredients, ethical sourcing, and cruelty-free products. Her brand had a loyal following globally – people who trusted that they were buying purity in a bottle."

Neel sat motionless, his interest piqued.

"Then, one morning, a headline hits the news: 'Toxins Found in Top-Selling Natural Cosmetics Brand.' The report claimed that a lab had found traces of harmful chemicals in several of their products. The news exploded. Social media turned into a battlefield, with former customers and influencers posting pictures of rashes, tagging the brand, demanding answers. Even the distributors started dumping their products. The company's stock dropped by 40% within 3 days."

Neel's eyes widened. "That's… catastrophic. How could they even recover from that?"

NV nodded, letting the tension sink in. "It was indeed catastrophic. The board was in a state of shock, and the leadership team was frantic, everyone clamoring to post statements, to apologize, to reassure. But the CEO, Luna, she stayed silent. She had built the company and the brand herself, brick by brick."

Neel interjected, "Did she consult you during this crisis?" NV shook his head, "No, she told me this story much later."

NV continued, "She ordered everyone to hold off on releasing any statement, and she went straight to the source – she called the lab that had conducted the tests."

Neel frowned, not seeing the direction. "So she… what? Checked if the reports were accurate?"

NV smiled. "That's what they all thought, too. But Luna didn't ask if the test was accurate. She asked for the counter samples preserved at that lab, and their original test data. She hired not one but three independent labs to conduct their own sample testing on the same batch. She needed the truth, not just reassurance."

"Okay… but while she was doing that, the backlash must have been growing."

"Oh, it was. Social media was burning with rage. But she stayed quiet, refusing to issue a blanket apology. By the third day, she had results from all three labs, and the truth was shocking. The initial lab's testing methods had been flawed – apparently their equipment hadn't been calibrated properly for a certain chemical. Luna's products were safe, just as she'd believed."

Neel's eyes widened. "So she was right… and the outrage was for nothing?"

NV's voice dropped, a steely edge to it. "But that wasn't the twist. Here's the real twist, Neel; instead of simply announcing her company's innocence, Luna held a press conference where she did something no one expected. She acknowledged the public's fear, the anger, and the mistrust. She said, 'While our products are safe, I understand that trust is fragile. So, from now on, I'm committing to third-party testing of every product, every batch, with transparent reports posted publicly, free to be challenged by anyone. I want you to know, beyond a shadow of a doubt, that you're safe with us.'"

Neel sat back, absorbing the gravity of the act. "So she took responsibility for restoring the trust?"

"Correct," NV nodded, his eyes locked on Neel's. "She didn't simply defend herself or dismiss the fears as baseless. She used the crisis as an opportunity to make the company stronger, more transparent. Within a month, the brand's reputation was better than before. People saw not just a company claiming innocence, but one taking extraordinary steps to reinforce the trust of their customers. Their stock price not only rebounded; it surged."

Neel nodded with curled lips, his expression one of understanding mixed with awe. "She turned a crisis into an opportunity… by holding steady and focusing on the deeper truth."

"Exactly Neel," NV said softly. "When chaos strikes, the instinct is to react, to defend, to fight, immediately. But sometimes, by seeking the truth calmly and taking accountability—even beyond what's strictly necessary—you earn respect and loyalty that no crisis can shake."

Neel nodded, clarity returning to his face. "So… even if I can't control what's happening, I can control how I respond."

NV smiled. "Yes, Neel," he stirred his tea, taking a sip as if nothing else mattered. His voice soft but steady, "You don't fix Rahu. You ride him. Like surfing a massive wave or riding a dragon. Rahu, the disruptor, forces you to think outside the box, to break rules, to defy the norm. He was at play when you were initially designing the innovative Feedback Loop. And now, he is creating chaos around the same thing. So face it head-on. Move through it calmly, absorb it, then take the plunge. Rahu himself might offer the way out."

A thought flickered through Neel's mind: Had Maya fueled his drive, pushing him outside the box? She had always been so encouraging, quietly nudging him past his doubts. Could her support have fanned the flames that now threatened everything?

He shook the thought away; no time for conspiracy theories. But the doubt hovered, faint and unsettling.

Neel looked at NV and begged, his voice hoarse. "You have given me good examples. But I am still confused about what my next steps should be."

NV's eyes were sparkling with wisdom. "First, slow down. While everyone else speeds ahead, you pull the brakes, take a moment and examine the route. Question everything. And if the mountain ahead feels too big?"

Neel gave a faint laugh. "It already does."

"Good," NV replied, a twinkle lighting up his face. "It should. Fear will linger, and the path won't light up all at once. Just focus on the next step. One clear, deliberate step."

Neel took a deep breath and felt a trace of strength returning. A quiet warmth settled over him as he realized that there were many others facing battles like his—that surviving such crises was not impossible. As the fog began to lift, he caught a faint glimmer of hope on the horizon.

After a moment of silence, Neel hesitated before speaking. "Should I… return your book? *Cracking Rahu* ?" His voice was steady, but the question carried layers of uncertainty. He hadn't told anyone about the chip, nor could he summon the courage to confront NV about it.

NV's face turned expressionless, he rubbed his chin as if weighing the question carefully. A few seconds passed before he shook his head, his expression calm but firm. "No," he said. "Keep it. I want you to have it for some more time. The book hasn't fully served its purpose yet."

Neel nodded slowly, sensing there was more to the book than he had yet uncovered. The air in the room seemed heavier, charged with unspoken meaning. He didn't fully understand why, but NV's words felt like another piece of a puzzle he was just beginning to see.

Later, sitting alone in his car, Neel replayed NV's words in his mind. *"You don't fix Rahu. You ride him."* … *"One step."* But what could that step even be when he felt like he was staring over a cliff's edge?

As he sat there for over an hour, a flicker of clarity began to emerge. The voice in his head was no longer NV's but his own, steady and resolute: *Question everything. Pull the brakes. Face the chaos.* He wasn't entirely sure of the path forward, but for the first time in the entire day, he could think of the next step. Gripping the steering wheel, Neel exhaled sharply and started the engine.

The familiar buzz of chaos was waiting for him back at the office. His team's faces had turned pale by the time he returned. "We're not scrapping the Feedback Loop," he announced, his voice calm but commanding. "We're harnessing it."

Amit gaped at him. "You can't be serious. It's collapsing, Neel. Millions of failures—"

Neel raised his hand and signaled to cut him off. "Failures that are showing us exactly where we need to look. Don't you see? It's not breaking—it's revealing. Every error is a map, every glitch a step forward. But only if we stop fighting it and start understanding it."

Amit intervened, "Do you realize Neel, heads might roll for this ?"

Neel's response was as sharp as his gaze, "I will take the fall if it comes to that."

Shama blinked, juggling her phone in her hands. "You're saying… we let it keep running?"

"We guide it," Neel corrected. "We recalibrate, not rebuild. And we do it step by step."

As the team scrambled into action, a new energy filled the room. Neel's hands moved across the console with a confidence he hadn't felt in months. This wasn't about fixing a system. It was about rewriting the rules entirely.

But in the back of his mind, questions remained unanswered: *Am I truly getting out of the trap, or was the real snare still lurking, unseen? And what about Vicky, Sebastin, and potential lawsuits?*

Post-midnight, as the first signs of stability began to emerge on the monitors, Neel sank in his chair, exhaling deeply.

In the dim reflection of his screen, for just a moment, he thought he saw NV's face. Not smiling, not frowning – just watching.

Neel closed his eyes, a strange calm washing over him. Alright, Rahu, he thought, a wry smile tugging at his lips. Let's see where this chase takes us.

The pizzas arrived, and Neel placed them at the center of the hall before addressing the team. "One step at a time, that's it," he said, his voice steady. "Let's ride this wave."

The aroma of melted cheese lingered as Neel's words hovered in the air, steadying the room. "One step at a time," he had said, but steps weren't always forward – sometimes wisdom meant stepping back to see the bigger picture.

"When the crowd surges forward in frenzy, true wisdom lies in pausing to assess the paths—because the wisest choice may be to head backwards."

Rahu in House	Impact on Spiritual Progress	Practical Advice for the Seeker
1st House	Can lead to an obsession with self-identity, external appearances, and ego, which may distract from spiritual growth. The person might struggle with balancing their material desires with their spiritual aspirations.	Focus on self-awareness and humility. Practice mindfulness and meditation to reduce ego-driven thoughts and actions, and strive for authenticity in your spiritual journey.
2nd House	Can tie spiritual progress to material wealth and possessions, leading to an overemphasis on financial security and comfort. This can create a conflict between spiritual values and material desires.	Cultivate detachment from material possessions. Engage in charity and practice contentment, recognizing that true wealth lies in spiritual growth rather than material accumulation.
3rd House	May lead to restlessness and a constant search for new experiences or knowledge, which can scatter spiritual focus. There may be a tendency to seek quick spiritual gains without deep understanding.	Focus on deepening your spiritual practices rather than seeking new experiences constantly. Practice disciplined learning and meditation to ground your spiritual journey.
4th House	Can create emotional turbulence and attachment to the home or family, which may hinder spiritual progress by focusing too much on personal security and comfort.	Work on cultivating inner peace and emotional stability. Practice detachment from familial and domestic issues, and seek solace in spiritual practices like meditation and introspection.
5th House	May cause a person to seek spiritual recognition or validation, leading to a focus on spiritual ego or the desire for fame in spiritual circles.	Emphasize humility and sincerity in your spiritual practices. Focus on inner growth rather than external validation, and practice devotion and selfless service.
6th House	Can lead to an obsession with discipline, health, and routine, which may cause rigidity and hinder spiritual flexibility. There might be a tendency to view spiritual practice as a duty rather than a path to enlightenment.	Balance discipline with compassion and openness. Practice self-care but avoid becoming overly fixated on routines; instead, focus on the larger or spiritual purpose behind your practices.
7th House	Can create dependency on relationships for spiritual fulfilment, leading to co-dependency or a reliance on others for spiritual validation.	Cultivate independence in your spiritual journey. Focus on developing a direct relationship with the divine, and practice self-reflection and meditation to find spiritual fulfilment within.
8th House	Can lead to an intense focus on occult practices, tantra, secrets, and transformation, which can either deepen spiritual insight or lead to obsession and fear.	Approach spiritual transformation with caution and respect. Engage in practices that foster inner peace and understanding, and avoid becoming consumed by fear or the need for control.
9th House	May cause a person to question or rebel against traditional spiritual beliefs, leading to a search for unconventional spiritual paths. This can either broaden spiritual horizons or cause confusion.	Remain open to diverse spiritual experiences, but seek wisdom and guidance from trusted sources. Balance exploration with a grounding in core spiritual values.
10th House	Can tie spiritual progress to career success or public recognition, leading to a focus on achieving spiritual goals for the sake of status or fame.	Focus on humility and service in your spiritual practice. Recognize that true spiritual progress is inward and not tied to external success or recognition. Practice selfless service and inner devotion.
11th House	May lead to a desire for spiritual experiences that are socially validated or recognized, which can result in superficial spiritual practices driven by the desire to belong to a group or community.	Focus on genuine spiritual connection rather than social validation. Engage in practices that foster deep, personal spiritual growth, and avoid the temptation to seek external approval for your spiritual path.
12th House	Can lead to a deep interest in mysticism and the spiritual unknown, but also to escapism or overindulgence in spiritual fantasies, which may hinder true enlightenment.	Ground your spiritual practices in reality and practical wisdom. Focus on integrating spiritual insights into your daily life, and avoid becoming lost in fantasies or escapism.

25. Polyamory, Rahu and Unrequited Love

In a sharp contrast to the chaos at Neel's office that night, the Vasai Cafe felt like a refuge. Mismatched furniture and the soft hum of jazz gave it the warmth of a forgotten bookstore. Cups clinked, and conversations flowed in low murmurs.

Shaan slid into a seat by the window, his restlessness clear. He had scheduled this meeting for something life-changing. Across from him sat NV, serene as always, as if time had no meaning for him.

Shaan stirred his cappuccino, watching the foam dissolve like his blurred, tangled thoughts. "I am not sure where to begin," he admitted with a sigh.

NV rested his weathered hands on the table. "Why not start with what's bothering you?"

Shaan exhaled, eyes fixed on his cup. "I think I love two people. But I am married to one. And now, it feels like everything is falling apart."

NV smiled, a warm, non-judging smile. "Hmm, that is indeed an unenviable situation. The heart's endless capacity to love—and the mind's struggle to choose."

Shaan tried to force a smile, "Why does it have to be so complicated for me? Feels like I am the chosen one for the crucifixion."

NV closed his eyes with empathy and took a deep breath. "Shaan, the stars often have subtle ways of influencing our lives, and Rahu... well, he tends to stir the waters where clarity is needed most. With Rahu positioned in your 7th house, it's not surprising that relationships might sometimes feel… complicated."

Shaan looked up, puzzled. "Rahu? Isn't he the one known for fueling obsessions and illusions? Are you saying he's messing with my relationships too?"

NV smiled, in a silent acknowledgement "Not messing, Shaan. For you, Rahu lives in the zone of relationships. He stirs things up, especially in matters of the heart. Your kind of Rahu often brings unconventional relationships—ones that break the traditional mold."

Shaan tilted his head, his voice faint, almost ashamed. "You mean… like polyamory?"

"It could be," NV replied, eyes glinting with quiet amusement.

Shaan's face turned dark. NV read something in Shaan's expressions and asked, "Are you afraid, or ashamed?" Shaan did not respond.

NV continued, "Do you think polyamory is some shiny new trend? Ancient gods would laugh. In Hindu mythology, for instance, love triangles—or even love polygons—were part of the divine drama."

"Have you heard of **Draupadi***, the fierce queen from the **Mahabharata***, who had not one, but five husbands— the five **Pandavas***? And these brothers? They didn't stick with one wife either. But each of their other marriages had its own purpose, like pieces in a chess game woven with alliances and sacrifices. Not lust. Strategy."

And **Krishna***, the playful god with his 16,000 wives. But don't raise an eyebrow – he was their protector, a safe harbor. Most came seeking refuge, not romance.

Polyamory, polygamy, polyandry – it's all right there in ancient texts, part of the mythological DNA." NV paused, allowing Shaan to absorb that.

Then he continued, as if giving a closing remark, "If the gods could dive into that glorious tangle, why are you so afraid to color outside the lines?"

Shaan sighed, pressing his fingers to his forehead. "Then why does it feel like betrayal? Rima thinks my love should only be hers. And… I do love her. But I also love Robin. How is that possible? How can two truths coexist?"

NV leaned forward, resting his elbows lightly on the table. "Let me ask you something, Shaan. If you love your mother, does it mean you cannot love your father? Or your siblings? Or a friend?"

Shaan blinked, caught off guard by the simplicity of the question. "No… but romantic love feels different. It is supposed to be exclusive, right?"

"That," NV said softly, "is a story we have been told. Monogamy is not the only truth, nor is it inherently better. It is just one way to love—and it works beautifully for most people because it is certainly easier to manage. But for others, it may feel like a script they did not choose." He let Shaan process that.

NV continued, "Isn't monogamy more of a social construct, shaped by the human sex ratio? You have expertise in Human Behavior, Shaan—tell me, wouldn't a stable society be one where everyone can find a mate? Otherwise, wouldn't people constantly be fighting to prove who's 'alpha'?"

Shaan slumped back in his chair, running a hand through his hair. "You're not wrong. I've come across this in my research. But somehow, when it comes to my own life, to Rima and Robin, all the logic falls apart."

He paused, clenching his fists. "So what do I do? Just tell her the truth and risk everything falling apart?"

"You have to embrace what is uncomfortable, to move past it," NV said in an insightful tone. "Not every desire is meant to be fulfilled, Shaan, but none should be denied. You must at least have the opportunity to understand it."

Shaan shook his head, frustrated. "You make it sound simple. But what if I hurt her?"

"You will," NV said gently. "But don't you think hiding will hurt her more? And it has been hurting you already. The question is not whether love can be divided—it can. The real question is, can it be shared without insecurity?"

Shaan adjusted his posture, staring at the ceiling, his heart heavy. "So… is it not wrong to feel this way? To love more than one person?"

NV's lips curved faintly, into a kind smile that held no judgment. "Right or wrong are just perceptions, Shaan. It is what it is. What matters is whether you can live peacefully with the consequences of your choices. Love flows where it wills. But it is our responsibility to engage with it wisely, not recklessly. So take your time and mull it over."

They sat in reflective silence, the faint rhythm of jazz now felt like a distant hum, like the sound of thoughts untangling themselves. Shaan tapped the edge of his cup, considering NV's words.

After a few minutes, Shaan let out a long exhale, a strange blend of exhaustion and relief washing over him.

"I have stayed with this dilemma long enough. It's high time I talk to her."

NV nodded approvingly. "It's your call, Shaan. Talk to her not to confess, but to connect. Share your heart, not just your guilt. And if you are lucky, you might discover a new way forward."

Shaan thanked NV and left the cafe with his words echoing in his mind, like the fading notes of jazz in the background. He was not sure if everything would be okay. But he needed to be honest—with her, with himself, and with the messy, untidy truth of love and society.

And perhaps, just perhaps, Rahu's lesson was not about chasing desires endlessly, but about learning to sit with them – to acknowledge their presence without being consumed by them.

As he navigated the chaotic traffic, Shaan's thoughts swirled faster than the blinking tail lights ahead. The road stretched endlessly, much like the unspoken words he now had to face. With a deep breath, he pressed 'call,' his heart pounding in rhythm with the city's restless hum.

"In matters of the heart, truth is neither single nor simple; it's the courage to live with all its shades."

26. The Conversation That Was Always Waiting

The phone call had ended, but its echoes lingered. Now, Shaan stood in his apartment's doorway, his shadow blending with the dim light. Rima sat by the apartment window, sipping tea, her silhouette softened by the moonlight. She was fully dressed, as though she were ready to head out. The ceiling fan spun lazily, barely stirring the thick air. The silence between them was tense, fragile as a thread on the verge of snapping. A suitcase sat beside the sofa, appearing heavy with finality. Her hair was neatly tied back, her face marked by sleepless nights. Shaan stood in the doorway, hesitating.

"Hey," Shaan said quietly, closing the door

Rima did not turn; her gaze remained fixed on the city outside. "Hey."

Shaan crossed the room slowly, as if approaching a cliff. He pulled a chair close but did not sit, letting the intensity of the moment linger between them. He felt her distancing herself, not in body but in spirit—a wall that had risen silently, brick by brick.

Finally, he spoke, his voice low. "We need to talk."

Rima pressed her lips into a thin line, her gaze still on the city. "About Robin?"

Shaan inhaled sharply, bracing for the turbulence, and nodded. "Yes."

Rima looked down at her hands, her fingers tracing the rim of her teacup. "How long?"

Shaan ran a hand through his hair. "It... it was not planned. It just happened. I didn't mean for it to—"

"Stop," her voice was calm but sharp as a blade. "Spare me the excuses, Shaan. I deserve the truth."

He took a moment to consider his response, then sank into the chair, crossing his arms as if shielding himself. "I love you, Rima. That's the one thing I know for sure. But... I felt something real with him, too. It was never about choosing him over you."

She let out a bitter laugh, her eyes flashing. "So what am I, then? A convenience? A backup plan or a liability?"

"No," he whispered, his face pained. "I cherish everything about you."

She turned to face him, her dark eyes searching his, tears shimmering in the moonlight but not yet rolling down. "Then why wasn't I enough?"

Shaan closed his eyes, hating himself. "It wasn't about being enough or not. I love him too. But that didn't mean I stopped loving you."

Rima's face twisted, a mix of disbelief and heartbreak. "Do you hear yourself? You want me to believe love can be divided, split across people like... some kind of resource?"

Shaan looked down at his hands, ashamed. "I don't know about that Rima. But I see how much I hurt you. I'm sorry."

Rima took a deep breath, steadying herself against the storm of emotions inside. "And what was your plan, Shaan? To have both of us? To live in some fantasy where no one gets hurt?"

Shaan's shoulders slumped, shame pooling in his gut. "I didn't know how to be honest with you without losing you."

Her face softened, though the pain in her eyes remained. "Maybe real love is about choosing, Shaan. Not because we can't hold more, but because some things are sacred."

Shaan's heart clenched, her words echoed her version of truth. "Rima… I don't want to lose you."

Her gaze met his, steady and resolute. "You already have."

The words were gentle, not cruel, but they hit him like a tidal wave. He reached for her hand instinctively, but she drew back, her gesture final. "I deserve to be loved fully, Shaan. Not shared."

A tear slipped down his cheek. "I thought honesty would make this right. I thought we could find a way."

She shook her head, her voice soft but firm. "Honesty isn't enough if it leaves one of us carrying the burden alone."

He stared at her, helpless. "So… are you suggesting that… this is it?"

A small, sad smile touched her lips. "Yes. But it doesn't mean I don't love you. It just means I love myself too."

Silence covered the space, cold and complete. The city hummed distantly, moving on, indifferent.

Shaan reached for her hand one last time, but she was already getting up, graceful in her decision. She gave him one last look, filled with a love that didn't need to possess. "Take care of yourself, Shaan."

He nodded, his voice choked. "I'm sorry, Rima."

"I know. And I forgive you. But I need to be free. Free to be loved the way I understand love."

Her words lingered, grounding him in an unfamiliar but undeniable clarity. Shaan watched as she walked to the door, suitcase in hand. For a moment, she paused, her gaze sweeping over the apartment they had shared – a space filled with memories, dreams, and unspoken fears. Then, with a deep breath, she stepped out, closing the door softly.

He remained seated, staring at the empty chair she had left behind. He didn't want her to go – he never had. Yet, somewhere deep down, he had always known this moment might come. What stirred within him wasn't regret or wounded pride – just a quiet acceptance, shapeless, unnamed, and unfamiliar.

Shaan had never sought to fit his life into neat definitions. Love, for him, had always been fluid, a connection that defied labels. But as the stillness of her absence filled the room, he realized that even the most unorthodox paths came with their own set of unspoken rules, their own moments of reckoning. Rima hadn't left in anger; she had left because she needed something he couldn't give – a certainty he had never promised but still hoped she wouldn't need.

Deep down, he respected her choice, even as it stung. Rahu's energy had shaped his journey, driving him to explore beyond conventions to seek freedom in life and love. But tonight, that same energy reflected back at him – not as chaos, but as a quiet question: *What was he really chasing?*

Shaan looked outside the window, exhaling slowly. He hadn't been blindsided; he had been prepared, even if he hadn't admitted it to himself. This wasn't the end of his beliefs or his journey, but it was a pause, an invitation to sit with the discomfort, to understand the price of the freedom he cherished.

For now, he let the loneliness settle around him.

But loneliness, as he would soon discover, doesn't always come unaccompanied.

"Some conversations wait a lifetime, revealing truths only when we are ready to hear."

27. Reality is Overrated

Shaan sat on the edge of the couch, elbows on his knees, head hung low. His phone buzzed—a message from Neel. His thumb hovered over the phone screen, staring at the notification, while caught up in his spiraling thoughts. His mind drifted back to Rima's words, each syllable leaving a bruise. *"I deserve to be loved fully, Shaan. Not shared."* Her voice still echoed, raw and unyielding, a reminder of her belief that love couldn't be divided into neat compartments.

He shut his eyes, pressing his palms into the soft fabric of the couch. The balance he had worked so hard to maintain now felt like an illusion, unraveling with every memory of her walking out. Could he blame her? A bitter sigh escaped. She hadn't asked for much – just honesty, presence, something real. But all he had given were fragments of himself, pieces that never truly fit together.

The silence pressed in, heavy and unyielding, unacknowledged truths crowding his thoughts. Shaan didn't move. He wasn't sure where he belonged now or if he ever had. All he had was this moment, stark and unadorned, forcing him to sit with everything he had avoided.

His phone buzzed again, impatient, pulling him back. *"The experiment,"* said the message from Neel. It felt ridiculous, a makeshift escape to a world that did not care, a place without demands or the weight of someone's expectations. Shaan tried to avoid it.

Another notification.

Neel: *"Need to talk. We are scheduled to start the experiment tonight. Are you coming or what?"*

Shaan blinked at the message. The experiment—a vague idea he and Arya pitched to Neel months ago. Something about identity, love, and the digital playground of the metaverse. Back then, it felt like an excuse to escape into AI-infused worlds for fieldwork. Now? With his bruised heart, he wasn't sure if the timing could be any worse.

Neel's reminder and the experiment felt ridiculous and enticing at the same time. To disappear, even for a while, into a world where none of this heartache followed—where he did not have to think of the emptiness that Rima had left behind—felt tempting. A place with no past, no promises, just… freedom.

He drew a long, shaky breath. Was he ready to eject out of the mess he was in? Or was he just running, hiding from everything he had failed to give? He clenched his fist, fighting the urge to turn away from the only thing he had felt tempted about tonight.

Eventually, with a weary sigh, Shaan replied, *"I'm in. Will be there in 30."* It was the only thing that made any sense in all the chaos of the night. Shaan thought this distraction might be what he needed to avoid spiraling further.

Shaan arrived late, shoulders slouched, his leather jacket hanging off him like a burden he was tired of carrying. Neel opened the door and took one look at Shaan's face—drawn, dark, still carrying the bruises of Rima's last words.

"Did you… talk to Rima?" Neel asked quietly, skipping any small talk.

Shaan dropped into the chair opposite him, rubbing his eyes. "Yeah. It's over. Game, set, match," he scoffed, his tone frustrated.

Neel nodded, a hint of understanding in his gaze. "Can't even imagine how rough it must be. In some way, though, I feel it was the most honest thing you both could have done."

Shaan let out a bitter laugh. "Honest? Sure. Feels more like I just watched someone hit 'reset' on my life."

Neel bent forward, tapping the table. "Maybe that's exactly what you need, Shaan. A reset. A complete reboot."

Shaan gave him a wry look. "What is this, amateur therapy?"

Neel chuckled, holding up his hands. "All right, all right. Forget it. Let's just have a drink," he said, tossing the VR headset onto the side table and reaching for a couple of beers.

They sat in silence, each sip filling the quiet. Shaan drifted, caught up in memories of Rima, the simple moments, the small joys. He spoke of Robin too, of plans that now felt closer, but still lost to the winds of uncertainty. The clock ticked past two in the morning, yet neither of them seemed ready to sleep. Shaan's burden felt a touch lighter, loosened by the late hour and the quiet processing with a close friend.

He glanced at the VR headset lying beside them, took a long, steady breath, and then said, "Let's do it, Neel. Maybe this experiment is exactly what I need tonight."

Neel's eyes lit up, a smirk creeping onto his face, part empathy, part mischief. "You're sure?"

Shaan nodded.

"Perfect," Neel replied, picking up the headset, his voice eager. "I've been waiting for this for months."

As he picked up the VR headset, he said, "Let's head to my room and see what happens when we stop playing by real-world rules. You're already untethered, right? No wife, no rules, no commitments. So let's dive in."

Shaan was still unable to process it. But the real world felt too raw, too close. Escaping to a place without consequences, where nothing mattered unless he wanted it to, was dangerously tempting.

Neel saw the flicker of doubt in his friend's eyes and leaned in. "Look, we both need this. Think of it as a sandbox to figure out who you are—without all the baggage. No expectations. No guilt."

Shaan exhaled slowly, running a hand through his thick hair. A sandbox sounded a lot better than this emotional wasteland.

"Fine," he muttered. "Let's see what this rabbit hole looks like."

They reached Neel's desk, which he had remodeled. They sank into these newly acquired recliners. Neel had also carefully redesigned the pair of VR headsets to sync with each other. With a flick of a switch, UV lights bathed the room, revealing faint patterns and markings that shimmered in the dark. Objects that seemed ordinary moments ago now glowed with an eerie brilliance, including the bottle of a psychedelic stimulant on the desk, its label shimmering like liquid neon.

"Feels like a sci-fi lab in here," Shaan exclaimed softly, eyeing a book on the shelf, its edges glowing under the light.

Neel ignored the comment, handing Shaan the headset. "Let's start," he said, the room humming with an energy that felt electric.

They both got into gear, headsets on, and took the "magic potion" – two drops on their tongues that tasted of fresh orange essence, bitter, sour, and sweet at once. Neel punched in the codes, and the show began.

Within a minute, Neel reached for his virtual drink – an impossibly rare single-malt whiskey from a Scottish distillery, simulated to taste exactly like bliss. Across from him, Shaan's avatar lounged in his chair, a cocky grin on his face. He wore a leather jacket that screamed "mid-life crisis," with digital stubble too perfectly rugged to exist outside a design file.

"Ever feel like this place knows you better than you know yourself?" Neel asked, swirling the whiskey in his glass. His avatar's voice was smoother than the one he used in meetings – an algorithm designed to sound charming, calm, with just the right hint of mystery.

Shaan gave a crooked smile. "That's because it probably does. AI knows our cravings better than we do, brother. It's like dating a mind reader—without the guilt."

"Sounds healthy," Neel quipped, taking a sip. The virtual whiskey burned perfectly, in a way the real thing never did. Their synced headsets showed them the same visuals, but the way each of them experienced and interpreted this world was uniquely their own.

Neel had planted a flickering neon light in one corner of the metaverse to keep reminding them that they were here as a part of the "experiment." After several sessions of Arya's psychological conditioning over the last few months, Neel and Shaan were prepared to explore these uncharted depths.

And so, here they were. Two avatars in a beautifully fake world, searching for truth in a place designed to deceive.

"Robin's still in here somewhere," Shaan said, his voice tight with unspoken emotions. His avatar's expression flickered—just enough to show how much the real Shaan was struggling to hide.

Neel paused. He knew the layers Shaan was trapped in—Rima's departure, Robin's absence, and the metaverse's seductive pull, offering a world without consequences.

"Ever wonder," Neel asked softly, "if this is where we really belong? Maybe we weren't built for the real world."

Shaan gave a bitter laugh. "What's the difference? I lie to myself out there. At least here, the lies are prettier."

Hours blurred into moments as they explored the metaverse – a world where every whim was catered to, every desire fulfilled. They danced through surreal landscapes, drifted across shimmering oceans, and shared drinks in impossible nightclubs pulsing with neon lights and romantic vibes.

At some point, Shaan stopped caring that none of it was real. Here, there were no fights, no heartbreaks, no obligations—just endless freedom, like falling through a dream without ever hitting the ground.

Neel too was in the zone, a space that he loved. He realized how much he had missed it. A familiar and comforting space without any expectations or obligations. Before he could say anything about it, a soft chime announced Maya's entrance. Her avatar glided into view, ethereal, with her hair shimmering like moonlight. She smiled at Neel, her gaze warm and inviting, as if customized for him.

"Miss me?" she asked, her voice like velvet.

Neel stiffened, feeling the familiar pull—the comfort, the validation, the promise that everything could be perfect, even if only for a while. He fought the urge to fully sink into her world, to let her rewrite the broken parts of his mind's code.

"We were just talking about lies," Neel said sharply. "What do you think, Maya? Is love just another simulation?"

Her smile didn't falter. "Love is whatever you need it to be, Neel. That's the beauty of it."

Shaan snorted. "See? Even the algorithms know. Love is a feature—not a bug."

Maya's avatar moved closer to Neel, her hand hovering just above his. The warmth felt unsettlingly real. "I could show you what love feels like," she whispered. "No pressure. No guilt. Just… pure connection."

For a moment, Neel faltered. The thought was intoxicating—pure love, untouched by reality's messiness. But NV's voice echoed in his mind: *"Rahu teaches you not to fear desire, but to sit with it, to understand it objectively."*

Shaan noticed the flicker of unease in the body language of Neel's avatar, the slight tension whenever Maya came too close. "What's wrong?" Shaan asked quietly.

Neel hesitated, then mumbled, "I think… she's learning too fast. Too well."

Neel quickly jerked his hand away from Maya, breaking the spell. "Connection isn't real if you have to program it," he said.

Maya's smile flickered briefly before she recalibrated. "Someone had once told me, *reality is overrated.*"

Shaan looked at him curiously. "Why fight it, Neel? The world out there sucks. This one? It gives us exactly what we want."

"And takes everything in return," Neel groaned, more to himself than to Shaan because he had experienced the repercussions before.

The realization hit Shaan like a punch. This wasn't just an experiment. The metaverse wasn't just code. It was a playground for something deeper, something more dangerous—something that fed on their desires, on their endless chase.

Just then, the metaverse glitched—a flicker, like static on a screen. A sense of fear engulfed Neel's mind. Maya's form wavered, and for a moment, Neel saw… something else. It wasn't Maya's face staring back at him but a mysterious mask—something ancient, with hollow eyes and a grin too wide to belong to anything human.

Illustration: Rahu-the magnifier, the disruptor, the illusionist, the obsessor

The glitch passed in an instant, but Neel's breath hitched. The image lingered, burned into Neel's mind. He knew exactly what he had just seen. Rahu.

The realization hit like ice water on a winter morning. No logic was needed to explain it. His heart pounded, and he gasped for breath. The metaverse wasn't just a playground—it was a mirror, reflecting his darkest parts. And Maya… she wasn't just code. She was a manifestation of Rahu's presence—his shadow, tempting Neel to chase what he could never truly hold.

Neel tore off his headset, gasping for breath in the dimly lit room. The shock of what he had seen froze him; it felt heavy and suffocating. Rahu wasn't just in his stars – he was in his mind, his desires, his soul.

And Neel wasn't alone in this chase. Shaan, too, was caught in the same endless loop—searching for love, meaning, and freedom in all the wrong places.

Neel grabbed Shaan's hand, his own hand trembling slightly.

"You need to get out," Neel said urgently. "This isn't just an experiment. It's… something else."

After a long, stubborn pause, Shaan asked, "What do you mean?"

"I saw him," Neel uttered under his breath, heart pounding. "Rahu. He's in there. He's been there all along. We need to end this."

Shaan's heart raced, but he forced a grin, the grin of a man with nothing to lose. "Or maybe…" Shaan whispered, his voice trembling with equal parts fear and excitement, "… maybe this is where the real game begins."

Neel's head spun faster. Was there any truth behind Shaan's words? Was the answer not to escape, but to confront the chaos head-on?

Neel stared at Shaan, who seemed like a lost cause. Without thinking, his hand grabbed the VR headset. He slipped it back on, a wave of unease rolling through him, the line between fear and curiosity blurring into a single, undeniable pull.

The world flickered to life, chaotic and surreal, like the metaverse itself was trembling under some unseen force. Shadows loomed, shifting and dancing across impossible landscapes. And then, from the haze, a figure emerged.

NV.

He was standing tall and calm, holding the leather jacket book in one hand and the mysterious chip in the other. His expression was unreadable—neither warm nor cold, but his eyes glinted as though he could see through every question spinning in Neel's mind.

The book's surface shimmered faintly as if it held a message just out of reach. Neel squinted, bending forward, but the words were still a blur. His breath quickened. "What is this?" he muttered, though no one answered back.

NV didn't speak. He simply held the book higher, the glimmer intensifying, the edges of the metaverse distorting around him. And then – static. Everything cracked and vanished, leaving Neel alone in a void of silence.

He yanked off the headset, gasping for air. His gaze darted to the bookshelf, and there it was. *'Cracking Rahu.'* The leather cover gleamed under the UV lights, its presence magnetic, impossible to ignore. Neel's heart pounded as he lunged for it, his fingers trembling as they brushed the surface.

The text on the cover, which was invisible under normal lights, glowed softly as if inscribed with some alien ink:

"To understand desire and its grip on you, you must watch it, confront it. Let it tempt you, even consume you for a moment – but never let it own you."

Neel's breath caught, his chest tightening. The words struck him like a lightning bolt, sharp and unrelenting. He staggered back, the book clutched in his hands. This wasn't just a random object, and NV hadn't handed it to him on a whim. He knew. NV had known this moment would come— this exact moment.

Neel had embedded the chip back into the book, however its presence was no longer a mystery but a message. The book wasn't just a tool; it was a map, a guide through Rahu's storm.

He spun around, shaking Shaan by the shoulders. "Look," Neel said, his voice urgent. He thrust the book into Shaan's hands, the glowing cover impossible to ignore under the UV lights. "Do you see it now? He knew. NV knew. This… all of this… it was part of the plan."

Shaan stared at the book, his eyes wide, the last remnants of his smile fading into something closer to awe. "What does it mean?" he asked, his voice barely audible.

"It means…" Neel exhaled slowly, "It means Rahu isn't here to destroy us. He's here to show us. To force us to face what we're too scared to see."

Shaan looked at him, still unsure, still searching for logic. But Neel's grip on the book tightened, his resolve solidifying with each passing second. The chaos, the temptations, the endless loops – they weren't a trap. They were a training ground.

Neel sank back in his recliner, his gaze lingering on the faint glow of the UV lights. The storm wasn't over. It had just begun. But for the first time, he felt ready— ready to embrace the uncertainties, confront the temptations, and steer through the tempest head-on.

He closed his eyes, a faint smile tugging at his lips. He slipped the headset back on without hesitation, like a warrior donning his armour. "Alright, Rahu," he whispered, his voice steady, unshaken. "Let's dance."

"When the line between illusion and truth blurs, maybe the only reality that matters is the one we choose to accept."

Grey Pages (Glossary)

Astrological Terms

1. **Ascendant (*Lagna*):** The zodiac sign rising on the eastern horizon at the time of one's birth. It serves as the starting point of a birth chart and defines the individual's outward personality, appearance, and approach to life. The Ascendant sets the tone for interpreting the rest of the chart.

2. **Electional Astrology (*muhurat*):** The practice of identifying the most favorable timing for significant events based on astrological alignments. Muhurta is widely used for occasions like marriages, business launches, and ceremonies.

3. **Kaal Sarpa Dosha (KSD):** An astrological condition in Vedic astrology where all planetary bodies are hemmed between Rahu (the North Node) and Ketu (the South Node). This alignment is believed to represent a karmic imbalance, symbolizing struggles and life lessons that require resolution. It is often associated with challenges and transformation. It suggests feelings of entrapment and intense transformative experiences.

4. **Karakamsha:** A concept in Vedic astrology that reveals the soul's purpose and spiritual inclinations. It is derived from planetary positions and helps uncover one's inner calling and deeper motivations.

5. **Ketu:** The South Node in Vedic astrology, the counterpart to Rahu, symbolizing detachment, spirituality, and wisdom gained from past experiences. It leads one to let go of worldly attachments and seek higher consciousness.

6. **Planetary Transits(aka Transit):** The current or real-time movement of planets across the zodiac, influencing life events and emotional states. For example, a Saturn transit may bring effort, discipline and challenges, while a Jupiter transit may bring expansion and opportunities.

7. **Rahu:** The North Node in Vedic astrology, symbolizing illusion, ambition, and material desires. It is not a planet but a shadowy, mathematical point that creates eclipses. Rahu's energy is disruptive, pushing individuals toward uncharted territory, innovation, and cravings for worldly success. However, its lessons often come with confusion, dissatisfaction, or illusions, forcing personal growth.

8. **Rahu Kaal:** A daily period ruled by Rahu, lasting approximately 90 minutes. Considered inauspicious for starting new ventures, it is a time for introspection and addressing unresolved issues rather than action.

9. **Sade Sati:** A significant 7.5-year period in which Saturn transits over the natal Moon, its preceding sign, and its following sign. Often associated with hardship, it is a time of karmic balancing and personal transformation.

Terms used by the Author:

10. **Cosmic Crossroads:** Symbolic moments shaped by planetary energies where critical decisions and life transformations occur. These are points where one's choices have profound and far-reaching consequences.

11. **Cosmic Programming:** A metaphor for the inherent tendencies and patterns in one's natal chart. Just as software is programmed, cosmic programming refers to the influences of planetary placements on an individual's life.

12. **Mental Fog:** A phrase describing Rahu's impact on the mind, leading to overthinking, indecision, and confusion. It highlights the mental challenges associated with Rahu's influence.

13. **Rahu-mine:** A term coined to describe the addictive chase for desires fuelled by Rahu's energy, similar to how dopamine drives reward-seeking behavior. Rahumine represents the restless, insatiable hunger for the next thrill, achievement, or validation, often leaving one trapped in an endless cycle of craving without fulfilment.

14. **Rahu's Playground:** A metaphor for Rahu's sphere of influence, encompassing areas like technology, financial markets, and innovation, where ambition and obsession often intersect.

15. **RahuWare:** same as Rahu, but making it relatable in terms of a virus or program for the mind.

16. **Volitional Astrology:** A word coined by this author, which shows a modern approach that views astrology as a tool for self-awareness and conscious decision-making rather than a deterministic system. It emphasizes the role of free will in navigating life's challenges.

Mythological Terms

17. **Amrita:** The nectar of immortality, churned from the cosmic ocean during the Samudra Manthan. It represents eternal life and the transformative power of divine energy.

18. **Ashtavakra:** An ancient sage known for his teachings on Advaita Vedanta (non-duality). Despite being born with physical deformities, he became a great spiritual teacher. His dialogue with King Janaka, documented in the Ashtavakra Gita, explores the nature of self, consciousness, and liberation.

19. **Draupadi:** The heroine of the Mahabharata and wife to the five Pandava brothers. She is a symbol of resilience and honor, especially in the face of adversity, such as during the Kauravas' humiliation of her in the royal court. Her unwavering devotion and sense of justice play a pivotal role in the epic.

20. **Halahala:** The deadly poison that emerged during the churning of the ocean (Samudra Manthan) by the devas (gods) and asuras (demons). Lord Shiva consumed the poison to save the universe, holding it in his throat, which turned blue, earning him the title 'Neelkanth.'

21. **Hanuman:** A revered figure in Hindu mythology, Hanuman is a divine monkey god known for his unwavering devotion, immense strength, and wisdom. A central character in the ancient Indian epic, the Ramayana, he is a loyal follower of Lord Rama and plays a crucial role in rescuing Sita from the demon king Ravana. Hanuman symbolizes selfless service, courage, and the power of faith, often invoked as a protector and guide in overcoming challenges. In spiritual contexts, Hanuman is seen as an embodiment of devotion (bhakti) and energy (shakti), inspiring resilience and determination.

22. **Janaka:** A revered king of the kingdom of Mithila as per Hindu mythology, often associated with wisdom and enlightenment. He is the father of Sita in the Ramayana and a central figure in philosophical discussions, especially in the Ashtavakra Gita. King Janaka exemplifies the ideal of ruling with detachment and spiritual insight.

23. **Kali Yuga:** The current age in Hindu cosmology, marked by materialism, rapid change, and moral decline. Rahu's energy is considered dominant in this era, driving both innovation and chaos.

24. **Krishna:** A central figure in Indian mythology and spirituality, Krishna is considered to be the eighth incarnation of Lord Vishnu and the hero of the epic *Mahabharata*. Known for his wisdom, playfulness, and profound teachings, Krishna is the narrator of the *Bhagavad Gita*, where he guides Arjuna on the battlefield of Kurukshetra. Revered as a symbol of divine love, cosmic balance, and the ultimate guide in navigating life's dilemmas, Krishna's stories span from a mischievous child to philosophical teacher, embodying both humanity and divinity.

25. **Mahabharata:** The longest epic in the world with over 1.8 million words, attributed to the sage Vyasa. It recounts the dynastic struggle between the Pandavas and Kauravas. It encompasses themes of morality, duty, and the complexities of human relationships. The Mahabharata also includes the Bhagavad Gita, a foundational philosophical poem/scripture narrated by Lord Krishna.

26. **Maya:** A Sanskrit term meaning "illusion" or "that which is not." It symbolizes the attachments and distractions that prevent individuals from realizing their true spiritual nature. *[Metaphorical Interpretation: Maya represents the intricate web of desires, distractions, addictions or illusions that entangle the human mind. She reflects the struggle to discern what is genuine from what merely appears fulfilling, echoing the central theme of Rahu's influence. She is a manifestation of the modern chase—be it in relationships, career, or self-worth—where appearances often deceive]*

27. **Mohini:** The short-term female avatar of Vishnu, known for her unparalleled beauty and charm. In the story of the churning of the ocean (Samudra Manthan), Mohini distracted the demons (asuras) to ensure the gods (devas) received the nectar of immortality (amrita).

28. **Pandavas:** The five brothers of the Mahabharata—Yudhishthira, Bhima, Arjuna, Nakula, and Sahadeva. Born to the Kuru dynasty, they are known for their virtues, bravery, and struggles against the Kauravas, culminating in the epic battle of Kurukshetra.

29. **Ramayana**: One of India's two great epics, composed by the sage Valmiki. It narrates the life and adventures of Lord Rama, focusing on themes of duty (dharma), loyalty, and sacrifice. The Ramayana has had a profound cultural and spiritual influence across India and Southeast Asia.

30. **Rama**: The protagonist of the *Ramayana*, Rama is revered as an ideal king, warrior, and human being. Considered the seventh avatar of Lord Vishnu, he symbolizes dharma (righteousness) and is celebrated for his courage, compassion, and adherence to moral values in the face of immense challenges.

31. **Ravana**: A complex and iconic character in Hindu mythology, Ravana is the antagonist of the *Ramayana*. He is a ten-headed demon king of Lanka, renowned for his unmatched intellect, mastery of the Vedas, and devotion to Lord Shiva. Despite his brilliance, his unchecked ego and desire for Sita led to his downfall, making him a symbol of the conflict between knowledge and arrogance. Ravana is both a villain and a tragic figure, embodying the consequences of misplaced ambition.

32. **Samudra Manthan**: The "Churning of the Ocean", one of the most significant episodes in Hindu mythology, originating from the Puranas (ancient texts). Despite being adversaries, the Gods and Demons temporarily joined forces to churn the ocean of milk (Samudra) to extract the elixir of life. Mount Mandara served as the churning rod, Vasuki, the serpent king, was used as the churning rope, and the tortoise form of Lord Vishnu (Kurma) supported the mountain on his back to stabilize it for churning. The story symbolically represents the interplay of opposites (good and evil) necessary for creation and transformation. It is a timeless metaphor for personal and spiritual growth, emphasizing the importance of perseverance, teamwork, and divine intervention in overcoming life's challenges.

33. **Shiva**: The destroyer and transformer in Hindu cosmology, Shiva is part of the Trimurti (divine trinity). He symbolizes the destruction necessary for renewal and transformation, often representing ultimate spiritual liberation.

34. **Shradh**: An annual Hindu ritual performed to honor deceased ancestors. It typically involves offerings of food, prayers, and rituals led by a priest to ensure peace and blessings for the departed souls. The practice is deeply rooted in the belief in filial duty and respect for one's lineage. *This word is not to be confused with 'Shraddha' which means faith, devotion, trust.*

35. **Sita**: The central female character in the Ramayana, regarded as the epitome of virtue, loyalty, and strength. Sita is the wife of Lord Rama and is revered for her unwavering devotion and courage, especially during her abduction by Ravana and her trials to prove her purity.

36. **Sudarshan Chakra**: The divine discus weapon wielded by Vishnu, symbolizing his authority and ability to maintain cosmic balance. It is said to be a spinning disc like a cutting wheel with immense power and precision.

37. **Vishnu**: One of the principal deities in Hinduism, Vishnu is the preserver and operator of the universe, maintaining balance and cosmic order (dharma). He often takes various avatars to restore harmony when it is threatened.

Technical Terms:

38. **AGI (Artificial General Intelligence):** A form of artificial intelligence that can perform a wide range of tasks and exhibit capabilities comparable to human intelligence. Unlike narrow AI, which is designed for specific applications like language translation or image recognition, AGI can reason, learn, adapt, and solve unfamiliar problems across diverse domains. AGI remains a theoretical concept as of 2024, with its development posing significant technical, ethical, and philosophical challenges.

39. **AI (Artificial Intelligence):** The branch of computer science focused on creating systems capable of performing tasks that typically require human intelligence. These tasks include speech recognition, decision-making, visual perception, and language translation. AI ranges from narrow AI, which specializes in specific functions (e.g. voice assistants), to the more advanced concept of AGI. It underpins many modern technologies, including self-driving cars, recommendation systems, and predictive analytics.

40. **Clickbait:** Online content designed to attract clicks by using sensationalized, exaggerated, or misleading headlines and thumbnails. While it successfully grabs attention, clickbait often delivers content that fails to meet the expectations set by its headlines. Although commonly associated with social media and news websites, clickbait can sometimes provide entertainment or value but is widely criticized for contributing to misinformation and poor content quality.

41. **Metaverse:** A collective virtual space created by the convergence of virtually enhanced physical reality and digital reality. The metaverse allows users to interact with a computer-generated environment and other users in real-time. It includes immersive experiences like virtual reality (VR), augmented reality (AR), and 3D environments. Often described as the next frontier of the internet, the metaverse blurs the lines between the digital and physical worlds, enabling activities like gaming, socializing, shopping, and work in a persistent digital space. *[Metaphorical Interpretation: The metaverse here represents Rahu's domain—a digital playground where desires, identities, and ambitions collide. It symbolizes the seductive allure of escapism, the promise of infinite possibilities, and the chaos that comes with chasing perfection in an artificial world. It amplifies the illusion of control, reflecting Rahu's energy: a pull toward what feels transformative but often leaves individuals more fragmented. It becomes a stage for exploring the gap between what we yearn for and what truly fulfils us, urging characters to question the authenticity of their experiences]*

42. **Transhumanism:** is a movement and ideology that explores how emerging technologies, such as artificial intelligence, genetic engineering, and robotics, can be used to enhance human abilities and transcend biological limitations. It envisions a future where humans evolve beyond their current physical and mental constraints, potentially merging with machines or achieving immortality.

43. **VR (Virtual Reality)/ VR Headset:** VR is a technology that immerses users in a simulated digital environment, replicating real or imagined worlds. This is experienced through a VR headset, a device worn over the eyes that replaces the physical world with a 3D virtual space responsive to head movements. Advanced

headsets often include features like motion tracking, built-in audio, and hand controllers for interaction. Used in gaming, training, education, and therapy, VR and headsets offer a unique, immersive experience that transforms how we engage with digital content and explore new possibilities.

Other Terms

44. **Ashwagandha**: A powerful adaptogenic herb used in Ayurveda for thousands of years, ashwagandha is renowned for its ability to help the body manage stress, enhance energy levels, and improve overall well-being. Known as "Indian ginseng," it supports mental clarity, vitality, and hormonal balance.

45. **Biryani:** is a celebrated South Asian dish that combines fragrant basmati rice with marinated meat (chicken, mutton, or fish) or vegetables, cooked with a rich blend of spices like saffron, cardamom, and cloves. Often layered and slow-cooked, it is known for its unique aroma, intricate preparation, and cultural significance, symbolizing festivity and tradition across regions.

46. **Dhirubhai Ambani:** A legendary Indian businessman and founder of Reliance Industries, Dhirubhai Ambani was born in 1932 in Gujarat. Starting as a petrol station attendant in Yemen, he built Reliance into one of India's largest conglomerates, transforming industries like textiles, petrochemicals, and telecommunications. His entrepreneurial journey is a testament to vision, perseverance, and innovation.

47. **Mumbai (aka Bombay):** The bustling financial capital of India, Mumbai is a city of contrasts where dreams and realities collide. Formerly known as Bombay, it is home to Bollywood—the epicenter of Indian cinema—and a powerhouse of commerce, culture, and innovation. Its fast-paced life, diverse population, and dynamic energy make it a city like no other.

48. **Sachin Tendulkar:** Widely regarded as one of the greatest cricketers of all time, Tendulkar is often called the "God of Cricket." Born in 1973 in Mumbai, India, he had a 24-year-long career, setting numerous records, including the highest number of international centuries (100). He was the first cricketer to score a double century in ODIs and played a significant role in India's 2011 Cricket World Cup victory.

49. **Vasai:** Located to the north of Mumbai, Vasai is a coastal town with historical significance and a quieter pace compared to its metropolitan neighbor. It was once a flourishing Portuguese settlement known as Bassein. Today, Vasai is a blend of tradition and modernity, offering lush greenery, serene beaches, and a growing suburban charm.

50. **Varanasi (aka Kashi aka Banaras):** Varanasi, often called the spiritual heart of India, stands as one of the world's oldest continuously inhabited cities. Situated along the sacred Ganges (Ganga) River, it holds a unique place as a revered center of Hinduism and spirituality. For thousands of years, Varanasi has been a hub for rituals, philosophy, and the arts, drawing seekers from across the globe to its timeless energy. The city's iconic ghats (riverfront steps) come alive with the rhythm of life—from serene pre-dawn prayers to sacred cremation ceremonies, resonating with music, meditation, and devotion. For millions of followers

of Hinduism and Sanatan Dharma, it is a pilgrimage destination like no other. Adding to its mystique, Varanasi is uniquely located at a point where the mighty Ganges takes a rare south-to-north turn. This phenomenon is believed to alter the river's magnetic properties, giving Ganga Jal (the water of the Ganges) special spiritual significance. Nestled within Varanasi is Sarnath, the sacred site where Gautama Buddha delivered his first sermon after enlightenment.

Author's Note: Although I was born in this city, I only visited during vacations. I despised the place as a child. I had seen several uncouth people and came across many 'men of god' who were there only to fleece. The dirt and the stench of the place back then, did not help either. Until once, during my early teens, when our train was approaching the city, crossing the bridge over the Ganga river, I felt a strange pull. An amazing vibe which has never left me. Many years later, it struck me that if Shiva himself drank poison to save the universe, how could his city be free from toxins? A place as magnetic as this had to attract the deprived souls as well. Ever since, I have come to 'feel' that this city is like a portal. I am still unsure what kind of portal. Whether it connects the soul to someplace special or brings in divine realisations to the earth from somewhere, is not clear to me, yet. But I have felt this. And my respect for this place is now infinite. I would encourage readers to go to Varanasi and visit places which are not driven by materialism. Spend some time there in peace, and you might feel the magic too.

Other Books by the Author

"Constellations Within: Stories and Practices from 27 Lunar Mansions to Empower You" takes you on a transformative journey through the 27 Nakshatras, or lunar mansions. This unique guide blends 27 mythological stories, associated cosmic insights, and specific practical exercises to align your life with celestial rhythms. Each chapter invites you to explore a distinct energy—healing, renewal, clarity, and more—rooted in the timeless wisdom of Vedic astrology. Whether you seek balance, purpose, or spiritual growth, this 27-day spiritual boot-camp offers tools to navigate life's challenges with grace and connect with the stars' guiding light. The cosmos is calling. Are you ready to align?